Cahill Cowboys

Texas's Finest

In the heart of America's Wild West,
only one family matters—the legendary Cahills.

Once a dynasty to be reckoned with,
their name has been dragged through the cattle-worn mud,
and their family torn apart.

Now the three Cahill cowboys
and their scandalous sister reunite.

With a past as dark as the Texas night sky, it's
time for the family to heal their hearts and seek justice....

CHRISTMAS AT CAHILL CROSSING
by Carol Finch—October 2011

THE LONE RANCHER
by Carol Finch—November 2011

THE MARSHAL AND MISS MERRITT
Debra Cowan—December 2011

SCANDAL AT THE CAHILL SALOON
Carol Arens—January 2012

THE LAST CAHILL COWBOY
Jenna Kernan—February 2012

Author Note

Welcome back to Cahill Crossing!

I am pleased to present my debut novel, *Scandal at the Cahill Saloon*. I hope you find the same enjoyment in reading it that I did in writing it.

In *The Lone Rancher*, Carol Finch presented us to Quin Cahill, the oldest Cahill brother and a man determined to hold the 4C ranch and the Cahill legacy together. In *The Marshal and Miss Merritt*, Debra Cowan gave us Bowie Cahill, the second-born son, a lawman determined to bring whoever is responsible for their parents' deaths to justice.

In *Scandal at the Cahill Saloon*, book number three of the Cahill Cowboys series, I introduce Leanna Cahill, the youngest child and only sister. Come with me and discover how Leanna goes from being the spoiled darling of the family to a woman with the strength to defy a town and to help women who society deems ruined. Be there when she finds her hero in gambler Cleve Holden. Together, they will continue the quest to discover who murdered Earl and Ruby Cahill. Travel with them while they tumble into love and while they help fallen women find a better life.

Working on this project with Carol Finch, Debra Cowan and Jenna Kernan has been a fabulous experience. A dream come true, really, for a newly published author. Occasionally I need a pinch to be sure this has really happened.

Find out why the Cahills are Texas's Finest in *The Last Cahill Cowboy* by Jenna Kernan, the final book of the series.

Thank you and enjoy,

Carol

CAROL ARENS

SCANDAL AT THE CAHILL SALOON

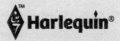

TORONTO NEW YORK LONDON
AMSTERDAM PARIS SYDNEY HAMBURG
STOCKHOLM ATHENS TOKYO MILAN MADRID
PRAGUE WARSAW BUDAPEST AUCKLAND

Recycling programs
for this product may
not exist in your area.

ISBN-13: 978-0-373-29671-2

SCANDAL AT THE CAHILL SALOON

www.Harlequin.com

Printed in U.S.A.

CAROL ARENS

While in the third grade, Carol Arens's teacher noted that she ought to spend less time daydreaming and more time on her sums. Today, Carol spends as little time on sums as possible. Daydreaming plots and characters is still far more interesting to her.

As a young girl, she read books by the dozens. She dreamed that one day she would write a book of her own. A few years later, Carol set her sights on a new dream. She wanted to be the mother of four children. She was blessed with a son, then three daughters. While raising them, she never forgot her goal of becoming a writer. When her last child went to high school, she purchased a big old clunky word processor and began to type out a story.

She joined Romance Writers of America, where she met generous authors who taught her the craft of writing a romance novel. With the knowledge she gained, she sold her first book and saw her lifelong dream come true.

Today, Carol lives with her real-life hero and husband, Rick, in Southern California, where she was born and raised. She feels blessed to be doing what she loves with all her children and a growing number of perfect and delightful grandchildren living only a few miles from her front door.

When she is not writing, reading or playing with her grandchildren, Carol loves making trips to the local nursery. She delights in scanning the rows of flowers, envisioning which pretty plants will best brighten her garden.

She enjoys hearing from readers and invites you to contact her at carolsarens@yahoo.com.

Scandal at the Cahill Saloon is Carol Arens's debut novel!

To my mother, Catherine Ebert, who snuggled me in one arm, my baby sister in the other, and read books to us.

And

To my father, Glenn Ebert, who was my first hero.

Prologue

Central Texas, early 1880s

Leanna Cahill closed the front door on the most awful hour of her life. Folks from neighboring ranches would soon be showing up with food, wanting to tell stories about Mama and Papa and trying to console the family's grief.

She wanted none of that. No amount of food or socializing could ease a whit of the emptiness she felt. The one and only thing she wanted was to drag herself upstairs and never come down.

Apparently, her oldest brother, Quin, had other plans.

"All right, Ma and Pa are gone, but they've left a legacy for us."

The signs of Quin winding up to a speech were all there. Leanna sat down on the couch in a flounce of black silk.

"We need to step up and run this ranch as a family, because that's what they would want. Pa talked about expansion and that's what I'm aiming for. We'll pour the profits from the ranch and the town rents back into the 4C. Bowie, your place is here now, with your family. I'm assigning you the raising, breeding, training and sale of the horses."

"I have a job, in case you've forgotten, brother."

What had gotten into Quin? He knew how set on law enforcement Bowie was. Leanna rubbed her puffy eyes. Sorrow weighed her down with the effect of a sedative. As soon as she could, she'd escape upstairs.

"You'll oversee the livestock and the hired hands, plus the daily running of the ranch operation," Quin continued as though Bowie hadn't even spoken.

"Annie, you'll be in charge of the household. Meals, staff, and supplies…everything that Ma did."

Since Quin was grieving, too, Leanna would allow for the fact that he might not be thinking straight. If, later on, the boys wanted to throw a party at the 4C she had the skills to play hostess. And really, Mama wouldn't exactly be proud of her domestic skills. She'd laugh a seam open in her brand-new heavenly gown if she looked down and saw her only daughter in charge of chores.

Mama left some big shoes to fill. Leanna would be lost in them.

"Chance," Quin went on, apparently unaware of

the rising resentment in the room. "You'll be second in command, working under me."

"So, I'm your hired hand?" Chance shoved his hands in the pockets of his suit pants and rocked back on his heels.

That would never work. Quin had to know that.

"Now, just hold on." Bowie stood beside her, his knee propped against the arm of the couch.

He didn't have time for Quin's job assignment and he told him so.

"Why do you have to go and change everything, Quin?" she asked. "We haven't even dried our tears yet. I need to go upstairs and bawl my eyes out, not go fix you something to eat. I don't want to be your housekeeper any more than Bowie or Chance want to be your hired hands." Leanna stood. She plucked at a wrinkle in her skirt. "Don't think I'm going to order the staff to get your supper, either. You can drag them from their grieving and order them yourself. Honestly, Quin, I'd rather move out on my own than let you take advantage of me."

"This isn't about what you want, Annie. It's about what's best for the 4C. We are a family and we stick together."

Quin didn't see it but his attitude was about to tear the family apart.

Bowie's scowl deepened by the second. Quin went on and on about duty and how Bowie should give up his calling since it was an unworthy one, anyway. A tick pulsed in Bowie's cheek, never a good sign.

Chance paced the room like Quin had shut him up in a cage.

"I'm a lawman," Bowie stated. "I'm not quitting my job to come back here and be your errand boy."

"Man up and do your part," Quin gritted out between his teeth.

Bowie shoved Quin against the wall. A bowl from Mama's wedding set fell on the floor and shattered. Leanna felt it slice her heart.

Quin shoved back at Bowie. He tumbled backward over the big leather chair that Papa sat in every night.

Bowie scrambled to his feet. "Go to hell and take your orders with you!"

Leanna stepped between them. She felt like she might be sick.

"Stop it!" She latched on to Bowie's flexing arm, then Quin's. "What do you suppose Mama and Papa would think of us? Can't this wait until—"

"Stay out of this, Annie," Quin ordered, then he railed at Bowie again, making all kinds of accusations.

Chance stepped away from the fireplace where he had stopped his pacing to watch the set-to between his brothers.

"We all have our dreams and they aren't the same as yours, Quin." Chance marched over to stand nose to nose with Bowie and Quin. "You aren't Pa and you never will be."

"We are doing what is best for the 4C," Quin enunciated slowly. He glared at his brothers, clearly daring them to say otherwise.

"Life has got other things for me," Chance declared, throwing back the challenge.

"Brother—" Bowie held Quin's gaze without flinching "—I don't answer to you anymore."

The three men Leanna loved most in the world were half a second from ripping the family apart. In the heat of grief and anger they could do and say things that might never be healed.

She stepped into the middle of the circle. Anger pulsing from each one of them struck her like a physical blow.

"No one made you ruler over us all, Quin!" she shouted, and hoped her desperation penetrated the violence ready to erupt.

It didn't. It only added fuel.

"Grow up," Quin growled at her. "You're not fit for anything other than looking pretty and playing games."

Bowie and Chance lurched into motion at the same time.

She said the one and only thing left to say. She uttered it barely above a whisper but it echoed like a gunshot. "I say we sell the ranch and each take our share."

Chance froze, his shocked gaze locking on her.

Bowie's head jerked toward her.

"Have you lost your damned mind?" Quin gasped.

Chances are, she had, but who in this room hadn't?

Quin was crazy with guilt, so were Bowie and Chance, for not having been with Mama and Papa that day. One of them should have been driving the wagon because of Papa's injured hand. His hand had to be the reason he lost control of the wagon. Any one of her brothers could have prevented that.

She tried not to judge them, but she couldn't… quite, even though her sin was just as great. At least her brothers hadn't done anything intentionally.

Leanna had been in control of every hateful word she had spoken to her mother when she and Papa had ridden away in the wagon that awful day. What kind of spoiled, shallow girl called her mother a… It hurt too much to bring up the word but it burned into her brain and seared her heart.

And all because Mama had said no to a new dress.

It had seemed so important at the time, to go to Wolf Grove with her parents and buy the prettiest gown in the dress shop for the family portrait.

If only she could throw herself into any one of her brothers' arms and let him make it all better.

Nothing would make this better, though, and she knew it. She probably did need to go her own way in order to heal and grow.

"Ma and Pa are buried on this land, you spoiled brat," Quin said in a soft, steel-laced tone.

Every one of them knew what that tone of voice meant. Quin had reached his limit.

Even though selling the ranch was the last thing she really wanted, Quin was right: she was a spoiled brat.

Now she had to get away, to show herself and Mama that she could make it on her own.

As it turned out, leaving wasn't as hard as she thought it might be. Quin, facing a mutiny, had given in to his temper and kicked them out. They each took only what they were wearing and their favorite horse.

Not a blessed one of them tried to get their oldest sibling to change his mind.

So Leanna rode away in a black silk gown on her black horse, Fey.

A hundred yards from the house, she kissed Bowie's cheek. After he rode away she kissed Chance's and gave him a hug. She promised to let both brothers know where she settled.

There wouldn't be much more communication than that, though. She needed to stand alone if she was to become a person she respected. She turned to look back at the house.

Quin stood on the porch alone. She wept then, for Bowie and Chance and even herself. Most of all she wept for Quin. All he'd wanted was to keep things the same and they had turned on him. He couldn't understand that nothing would ever be the same again.

Well, she couldn't turn back now, even if she wanted to.

"Let's hurry, Fey."

Clouds spread across the sky. A storm was coming.

Chapter One

August 1882

Leanna Cahill figured the good folks of Cahill Crossing might have forgiven her the sin of bearing a child out of wedlock were it not for the fact that she was managing quite nicely.

Indeed, had it not been for the tidy sum of cash that she had accumulated during her stay in Deadwood, they might have considered her afflicted and therefore worthy of their benevolence.

Bless their shriveled little hearts.

Coming home today for the first time in two years, she had no intention of being ashamed of either her child, her abundant funds…or the way she had come by them.

She lifted her chin and tweaked her best hat to shade her eyes from the glare of heat rising from the road in simmering waves. She tugged the brim of a tiny Stetson over her son's eyes, then hugged him close to her in the saddle.

The satin border of her gown, lying neatly across her horse's rump, winked purple flecks at the sky with the shifting of the animal's gait.

She could have crept into town, hiding in the shadows as though she were ashamed. Crawling on her knees, sackcloth and ashes style, might have made people look more kindly at her.

The plain fact was, she wasn't ashamed. Why should she be? The fifteen-month-old child snuggling into her, with his little boot-clad legs too short to even dangle over the horse's withers, was perfection.

He was as worthy as any Cahill had ever been. Anyone who tried to say otherwise would answer to her. Even her own brothers if it came to that, but it was her daily prayer that they would not hold the sins of little Cabe's parents against him.

Her dearest hope was to reunite with her brothers. It might not be possible; they had parted with hateful words and bitter accusations. Guilt and blame had torn them apart. It wasn't only their parents that had died that day two years ago; the whole family had been destroyed.

To add to the tragedy, it had taken Quin's telegram, with the awful news that Mama and Papa had not died by accident, to bring the family back to Cahill Crossing.

It made her sick, knowing that murder had been what finally brought her home. Not her bone-deep love for her brothers or even family loyalty...but murder. If it weren't for sly glances peering at her from every direction, she might dissolve in bitter tears for everyone to see.

Now, for good or ill, here she was. The ties of home wrapped her up. If she let everything about her fade to quiet, she could almost feel Mama's arms about her.

Even though she would have to be careful where Cabe was concerned, he deserved to be home with his family. Thankfully, he was too young to understand what folks whispered about his mama.

Just up the street a man and a woman strolled along the boardwalk. They didn't scowl at her, most likely because they were caught up in admiring the infant the woman cuddled close to her breast.

Leanna grinned, disguising her pain because she couldn't give her child that happy picture. She hugged his warm, solid little body closer.

She would be enough for him. Whatever his future held, she would be enough.

And he did have uncles. Now that she was home she would do her best to heal the rift with them and give Cabe the family he ought to have had all along.

In spite of the scorn she was enduring at the moment, she was glad that she had come home. With time, her brothers would come to love her boy as much as she did. In the end, family was everything.

Leanna glanced backward at the buckboard trailing fifteen feet behind. She waved. "Chins up, ladies, smiles bright!"

While her brothers might accept her child, she had doubts that they would be so welcoming of the four reforming prostitutes coming home with her.

At first sight, they did present quite a vision. While the ladies had determined to reform their behavior, their resolutions hadn't quite reached their manner of dress. Their gowns were proper enough to cover newly respectable bosoms, but feathers and gaudy be-bobs announced their former professions.

Leanna urged her horse past a new hotel in town on the way to her destination, Marshal Bowie Cahill's office.

The front door of the Château Royale opened and stylish Minnie Jenkins, who owned the place with her husband, Oscar, stepped out.

"Good afternoon, Mrs. Jenkins." Leanna nodded her head and smiled.

In years past, Leanna had been a welcome guest at the Jenkinses' home. Their daughter, Ellie, had been her closest friend. How many times had Mrs. Jenkins encouraged Leanna to set Quin or Bowie in Ellie's path? It would have been quite a social coup in Minnie's estimation for Ellie to land a Cahill.

Recently, Leanna had heard rumors about both of her older brothers being madly in love. That left Chance as the only Cahill male available. Minnie would have an apoplexy if Ellie ever took up with him. As a bounty hunter, his social standing might be almost as low as Leanna's.

Well, not quite, if the expression now crossing Minnie's face was anything to go by. The woman sniffed and pointed her dainty nose in the air.

Half a second later she noticed the reforming harlots in the buckboard. She pressed her hand to her chest as though she might faint dead away, but the scorn in her expression had enough starch in it to hold anyone upright.

Upstairs, second floor, in the corner window, a curtain moved. Ellie peeked out. Her friend was as pretty as ever, although she would never believe that of herself. Ellie waved her hand, but before Leanna could return the greeting the curtain dropped.

If Minnie had any say in it, and she would have, that was as close to Ellie as Leanna was likely to get.

Minnie Jenkins's rejection stung, but that was something she would have to get used to from her former friends.

Thanks to Preston Van Slyck gleefully spreading the word about her illegitimate son, Leanna's fall from grace had occurred well before she returned home. It was unlikely that she had a single friend remaining in a town that used to adore her.

She couldn't hide from that situation so she rode on, sitting as proud as she knew how and wearing her most dazzling dress.

As she had expected, not-so-secret glances from behind curtains and turned backs greeted her passing. One pinched-faced woman even spat on the sidewalk. As far as the citizens of Cahill Crossing were concerned, she was no better than the women following her in the wagon.

It was a lucky thing that little Melvin Wood, an abandoned boy that her fallen friends had taken in, slept soundly on the buckboard floor. A child of eight did not deserve the mean-spirited glances coming the way of the wagon.

Leanna led her entourage past the livery and the dry goods store, gathering ill wishes along the way.

She passed the law office of Arthur Slocum, the attorney who had handled the Cahill legal matters for as long as she could remember. Arthur, sitting outside and smoking a cigar, shot her the oddest look. It wasn't antagonistic, exactly, but it was something and it was not welcoming.

She had chosen her route and her attire for a very good reason. Gossip and whispers were bound to spread; at least by making her entrance a public spectacle she directed most of the attention to herself and away from her innocent little son.

The circuit through town was her announcement: here he is, a Cahill as worthy as any other.

Still, the ride couldn't end soon enough. Her cheeks ached with the strain of her forced smile. Her heart ached with the rejection of former friends.

With Bowie's office only steps away she let her expression fall.

She cast one more grin back at the ladies, but

that one was real, to give them encouragement. They needed to believe that *she* believed that their return to respectability was possible. Her show of reassurance was important even though it was all show.

Now, facing Bowie's front door, she had nothing left. Her heart beat triple time in her chest. Her palms grew damp gripping the horse's reins. Would he look at her as everyone else had?

If he did, her heart would split down the middle. She might begin to sob and thoroughly ruin her grand and scandalous parade through Cahill Crossing.

The front door opened and Bowie's deputy stepped out. He squinted at her through the bright sunlight.

Glen Whitaker arched his brows. His chin jutted out so that his narrow beard pointed at her like an accusing finger.

"Well, look here! See who's come home with her tail between her legs." He spat on the ground, but the effect of that gesture had long since lost its shock.

"Please send my brother out." She smiled as sweetly as she could manage. In the past this expression had sent men running to fulfill her merest whim.

"He's not here." Whitaker dragged his sleeve across his sweating brow. "Even if he was, he wouldn't want to see you or your bas—"

"Don't say one more word, Glen." She leaned forward in the saddle. She covered her son's ears with her fingers. "It's been a difficult day. Don't test me."

"I'm scairt now."

"You ought to be." This time she glared at him. In

the recent past, this expression had gamblers backing away from her poker table, ashamed of suggesting that she might want to make some extra money upstairs. "This little fellow is a Cahill, just like me, just like my brothers. I'd be careful about insulting him."

Glen opened his mouth but Leanna cut off whatever he had to say since it likely wasn't "Welcome."

"Have you ever run across an angry mama bear, Deputy?" He nodded and shrugged. "She can't shoot a bug out of the air, but I can. I learned that from my brother, Chance, in case you hadn't heard."

Evidently, he had heard. He tugged at his shirt collar and backed into the office, slamming the door behind him.

Leanna led her horse and her ladies away from the business area of town, toward the residential area where she had rented a secluded home for her and her son.

"We're home, Boodle." She hugged him closer. "Heaven help us."

The next day, Leanna decided she was blessed, helped by heaven, to be sure.

"It's perfect," she whispered, standing alone in the street, gazing up at the three-story building she had purchased sight unseen before she left Deadwood.

The Realtor had promised that the structure, a former home for railroad employees during the rail line construction, would suit her needs to perfection.

"Wonderful," she added in awe, still amazed at how well it did suit her needs. "All we need is a big, fancy stained-glass window right here in front."

The porch would fit half a dozen chairs. Inside, the ground floor was one big room, open wall to wall. The second floor contained five bedrooms. The next story was smaller to accommodate the slant of the roof but it had two more bedrooms and another open area between them.

Hearts for Harlots would be its unofficial name, though the sign over the door would read Leanna's Place, Gaming and Spirits for Gentlemen of Refined Taste.

"There's enough dust in here to stuff a pillow!" Lucinda Callet's voice carried through the open window on the first floor.

Lucinda was the first of her harlot friends from Deadwood to decide to change her life. She was a determined lady. Leanna was convinced that with the aid of Hearts for Harlots, she would succeed.

"That's to be expected." This voice belonged to pretty Cassie Magill. Only twenty-three years old, her new life stretched out before her full of hope. "Sweep it up and be grateful."

Leanna skipped up the steps of the front porch, her spirits much improved over yesterday. Grateful did not begin to describe how she felt.

The dream that she had held close to her heart for the past couple of years was coming true. Giving women a place to work and heal would be healing for her, as well. The ache in her soul that had never quite mended after her parents' deaths might ease.

During her time in Deadwood she had become another person. Grown from a child to a woman, really, in many ways.

Before Deadwood, before her parents died, life had been a party. Which new dress would she buy? Which boy would she charm? Which brother would be best for Ellie? Quin or Bowie?

But the family, as a loving unit, had died along with her parents. Angry words had cut wounds into broken hearts until the only thing left to do was flee. Everyone had done just that except Quin, who bore the responsibility of keeping the 4C going.

She had fled to rowdy, sinful Deadwood, and nothing would ever be the same for her again. She'd met women who, in her earlier life, she would have shunned, just as the folks in Cahill Crossing now shunned her.

She had learned to understand those women, to care for them, to respect them. Had it not been for the money that Chance had stuffed in her saddlebag while she kissed Bowie goodbye that last day, she might have been one of them.

The biggest change in her life had stolen her heart, every blessed beat of it. She had become a mother. She'd watched Cabe draw his first breath; his newborn cry had captured her. She would raise him to be as fine a Cahill as the family had ever known.

She could accept the loss of her good name. Her

little baby Boodle and her crusade to save women that society rejected made everything worthwhile.

A good reputation wasn't so much, anyway. It could mask all manner of deplorable behavior.

Preston Van Slyck was a perfect example of that. Here was a man who had the smile to charm. As the banker's son he was a social catch, every woman's dream. Leanna had good reason to know that underneath it all he was not.

Massie Monroe met her at the front door. Young Massie's story was a common one, as far as Leanna had been able to tell. She'd run away from home with a man her parents had disapproved of. When he'd left her high and dry she was too ashamed to go home and did what she could to keep from starving.

It was Leanna's personal goal to see that Massie did go home. It might take some time for her to gain the self-respect to do it, but with the help of Hearts for Harlots, she would.

"There's a load of goods just been delivered from the freight yard," Massie declared. Blond curls framed her face. She seemed the proper angel with her fair coloring and her soft voice. "There's a fellow out back who wants you to sign for it."

"This place is beginning to shine, ladies. At this rate we'll be open for business next week," Leanna said.

Out on the back porch two wagonloads of goods were being unloaded. She signed for them and watched while lamps, tables, chairs and chandeliers were carried past her and into her new saloon.

It was a lucky thing she had decided to dress like a man today. With all the heavy work, skirts would only get in the way. Years ago, on the 4C, she had often worn pants. Tagging along with Chance, or riding alone on the open range, it made sense. She had always respected her mother's wishes and never worn menswear to town, but her mother was gone and so was her reputation. There was nothing really to be lost by dressing sensibly.

Massie stepped onto the back porch and exclaimed over an exquisite red carpet being carried by two men. She followed them inside, admonishing them to have a care with it.

The young man waiting to take the papers from her hand stared after Massie.

"When are you opening?" he asked, not able to take his gaze off the door Massie had closed behind her. "I'd like to be the first for that one. I'll pay real good."

"You are welcome here anytime, but if you want those kinds of services—" Leanna pointed across the railroad tracks that ran a couple hundred yards behind her building "—I'm sure you know where to go. Pearl's or Monty's will take care of you. If you want a respectable game of cards, dealt by respectable women, you come back next week."

"Yes, ma'am. I'll be here." He shrugged his shoul-

ders, took the signed papers and gave one more long-
ing glance at the back door.

So far there was every indication that Hearts for
Harlots would send Massie home to her parents not
only respectable but married.

Sunset rolled in with a clap of thunder. Another
wagonload of crates had been delivered that afternoon, half of which remained unopened on the back
porch.

Leanna's back ached; her hands had grown red
and blistered. Sweet heaven, if her legs weren't as
weak as a newborn colt's.

Inky clouds toward the west snuffed out the last
rays of light. She lit a lantern beside the back door,
then plunked down on the stoop with a thud.

Crickets chirruped in the lilacs growing beside the
back wall of the building, fast and loud because of the
heat. A humid wind whistling in ahead of the storm
brushed her face and throat. She lifted a tangled hank
of hair off her neck to feel the air whisper over her
skin.

With darkness falling, the brothels and saloons
across the railroad tracks came to life. Lanterns
blinked on and pianos tuned up. Women's voices,
sometimes laughing, sometimes cursing, carried over
on the breeze.

How many of them, she wondered, hated their
lives? Mentally, Leanna designed the broadsheets
she intended to pass about in the red-light district

advertising Hearts for Harlots. Leanna's Place would be a haven, an escape for any woman who wanted it.

Her fledglings—Lucinda, Cassie and Massie—had gone to spend the night at the house Leanna had rented in the proper part of town, just until their own rooms above the saloon would be ready to live in.

Dorothy Wilmont had been at the house all day, caring for Cabe and setting the house to rights.

Dorothy was another whore from Deadwood. Older than the rest, she wanted nothing to do with saloons or the men who frequented them. Leanna had hired her to care for Cabe and keep house. She would need the help with all the hours she would have to spend getting her business running.

Rain pattered the back porch roof. It dripped off the eaves onto the dirt only a foot or two from where she sat.

Leanna filled her lungs with the fresh scent of damp earth.

Mama had loved the rain. It made everything cozy inside, she used to say. Papa hated it. Taking care of a ranch in the wet and mud made it a chore instead of a joy. He used to stare out the parlor window and growl about it until Mama took him by the hand and led him upstairs.

When they came down an hour or so later, Papa wasn't growling anymore.

"I'm sorry, Mama. I didn't need that dress." Leanna dug her fingers into her sore palms, regretting for the millionth time the argument she had had with her mama when they'd last parted. She wouldn't cry. She hadn't in some time.

But murder, Quin had said in his telegram. That made the grief fresh again, crueler and worse than before. Bowie, Quin and Chance would be itching to find out who did it, to make them pay.

They might try to keep her out of it, believing that she was still the baby sister who needed to be protected and coddled. They might try, but she had come home to see justice done for her parents and they would not be able to keep her from it.

"I know you can hear me way up there, Mama. I miss you."

Rain drummed on the roof harder now; it poured from the eaves, making pools in the mud. Lightning tripped over the buildings across the tracks, illuminating them one by one.

Smoke lifted from a kitchen flue on the roof of Landry's Boardinghouse. Wind blew the scent at her.

Apple cinnamon cake. The aroma drew her back over the years, into the kitchen of the 4C. She saw Mama smiling while she took a cake from the oven. Leanna was four…she was nine…she was fifteen, always bouncing up and down for the first slice of that warm cake.

Tears welled in her eyes. If she started to cry now she might not stop. She had a life to live. She needed to make Mama proud of her.

Leanna stood and dashed her sleeve across her

eyes. She grabbed a metal bar to pry the lid off of a wood crate.

The bar slipped. Her thumb jabbed the lid and a splinter gouged her thumb. Blood welled. Blood had streaked Mama's face in the mortuary in Wolf Grove.

Leanna braced her hands against the crate; she bowed her head, watching the crimson drops leak from her thumb. She cried as though the news of the deaths had just now been delivered. She sobbed her grief, her anger, while a red glob gathered on the porch.

"Miss Cahill?" came a man's voice from out of the dark, its tone deep and smooth.

She swallowed hard to smother her hitching breath.

Footsteps mounted the stairs. Wind groaned under the eaves as though it continued the mourning that she had abruptly halted at the sound of the stranger's voice.

"Here now…give me your hand," the voice said, seeming very close by.

"I'm fine." Leanna shoved her hand behind her back and turned to look up at the stranger on her porch.

Lightning flashed revealing a tan derby dripping water past warm brown eyes. The concern she read in them kept her from running into the building and locking the door like she should have. Like she would have, had her common sense not been bound up in grief.

Thunder stomped across the sky and vibrated the wood porch under her boots. The man reached behind her and drew her injured hand around front. He uncurled her fist, squinting at the wound in the dim light. He didn't seem to care that the cuff of his shirt absorbed a red smear.

He arched a brow at her. He might have been touching a wounded bird, his fingers were that gentle.

Drawing a handkerchief from his nicely tailored suit pocket, he wrapped it around her thumb and pressed.

She winced and he let go. He unwrapped the handkerchief and held her thumb up to the lantern.

"Nasty splinter," he announced, turning the wound this way and that. He tilted his head, taking a close look at it, probing gently with his thumb.

Who was this man? She couldn't ask just yet; her throat still ached with emotion. But he was handsome.

The light swaying across his face by the swing of the lantern revealed dark brown hair with raindrops collecting at the tips. His clean-shaven chin was pleasantly shaped. No doubt, if he smiled, he would have the kind of mouth to captivate a woman, to make her sigh out loud. She'd seen the like before.

He was a gentleman, not a cowboy, but tall and muscular-looking just the same.

Leanna had been judging men's looks since she'd first learned to flirt. There were important things a woman needed to know, such as that a handsome smile did not mean a handsome heart. A dashing flash in his eye might mean danger as often as welcome.

This one did not mean her any harm, she judged. But he did have the advantage over her. Even though they were strangers, he knew her name and where to find her. She'd be wise to keep her wits about her and her legs ready to spring inside the building, just in case she had misjudged him, after all.

"Take a good, deep breath, miss."

She yanked her hand. Really, she could remove her own splinter.

He held her fingers as though he hadn't noticed her pull at all.

And there went his smile. She had guessed right. It was irresistible…and distracting. She let her fingers fall open in his palm.

Maybe it was the lamplight that made the mischievous crinkle at the corners of his eyes so appealing. In the harsh light of day, no doubt he would be just another man.

In a blink, he had plucked the splinter out and wrapped the handkerchief around her thumb again. She watched his fingers, long and lean, hold the cloth to the wound. He squeezed with the just the right amount of pressure to hold the pain at bay.

"You're no stranger to splintered thumbs," Leanna pointed out.

"Just to removing them from such a delicate

hand." There came that smile again, intimate, even though she didn't know his name.

"You are a flirt, Mr...?"

"Cleve Holden." He checked her wound. The bleeding had stopped so he returned the kerchief to his suit pocket and let go of her hand. "Sorry about that, the flirting. Bad habit of mine when I see a beautiful woman. And you are very lovely."

"You aren't an ordinary flirt, Mr. Holden. You're quite skilled."

"That last bit wasn't flirting, just the plain truth." A crease beside his mouth flickered.

Irresistible, to be sure.

"Is there something you wanted? I doubt that you showed up on my back porch in the rain by chance."

"There is something, something rather urgent that I need to discuss with you." He looked at her face, clearly studying swollen eyes that were, no doubt, redder than beets. A deaf man would have heard her sobbing a few moments ago. "Now doesn't feel like the right time. It can wait until tomorrow."

"I'd rather discuss it now."

He shook his head, then glanced about.

"What do you say I put these boxes inside and walk you home?"

"What do you say you tell me how you knew where to find me at this time of night?" He seemed like a decent man but she might be mistaken this one time.

He hefted a crate like it was made of paper. Muscles tensed and flexed; they shifted the fabric of his coat sleeves. She hurried to open the back door. She absolutely would not sigh…or let her heart flutter at this display of male brawn.

"Finding you was easy," he said with a backward glance. "You've got to know that you are the talk of the town, Miss Cahill. Everything you've ever said or done is, at this very moment, being gossiped about from one end of Cahill Crossing to the other."

That was no surprise, but Cleve Holden was. He knew that she was a fallen woman and treated her with respect, anyway?

She watched him carry crate after crate into the building. He closed the door after putting the largest and last one inside. He didn't appear a bit winded.

She would not by any means imagine that he was her knight in shining armor simply because he hadn't insulted her.

"You know that I'm a strumpet of the worst kind?" she reminded him.

"Is that what you see when you look in the mirror?" A frown shadowed his face, etching waves of fine lines across his forehead. "I'd wager not."

"I'm a mother. I'm not married. That speaks for itself." Drumming rain ate up the silence between them. "I'm opening a saloon."

"Things aren't always what they seem, are they, Miss Cahill?" For a long heartbeat, his gaze held her.

No one knew the answer to that question more

than she did. She wasn't entirely comfortable that he had asked it.

Before she had time for concern to settle in, he grinned. Lantern light cast a glint in his eyes that twinkled mischief, not malice.

Cleve Holden took off his coat and extended his elbow. "I'm walking you home whether you agree to it or not."

She didn't need his arm to walk home on or his coat to huddle under. But once in a while a woman needed a knight, and if his armor was shining, for that brief moment, life was sweet.

She ducked under his coat and took his arm.

With lightning etching the sky all around, they dashed out into the rain.

Chapter Two

The next morning Cleve stepped onto the front porch of the Château Royale, closing the door on an argument between the proprietor and her daughter. Leanna Cahill's name had been mentioned a time or two.

Everyone, it seemed, had something to say about Miss Cahill. One of the things he knew to be a lie. A few he guessed were likely lies. The rest were none of his business.

Sometime during the night the storm had blown over. Morning air filled his lungs. It chased away the foggy visions that had haunted him through the wee hours and left him restless.

Surely by the light of day the lovely Miss Cahill would not seem so appealing. Last night in the rain and the lightning, the distressed woman had touched him in a way he hadn't expected. No doubt, in harsh daylight she would no longer seem a lost angel, weeping and in need of protection.

The truth was, he hadn't traveled to Cahill Crossing to protect Miss Cahill.

Far from it. As soon as he concluded his business with her he would leave this fledgling town and try very hard never to think of her again.

If his discussion with her went as he hoped, he could be on the noon train out of here. Since he hadn't even bothered to unpack his bag, he could be gone as quick and smooth as a deck of cards being shuffled.

Cleve straightened his coat, adjusted his hat and walked toward the most wicked establishment ever to spring up on the right side of the tracks, according to the lady proprietor of the Château Royale.

He didn't know if that was true. He didn't care much, either. Leanna Cahill had something that belonged to him and he meant to take it back from her.

There was a letter in his pocket, tattered and worn with many readings. It had led him from home, a hardscrabble homestead, to one tawdry town after another. Finally, in Deadwood he had discovered that Cahill Crossing was where he would find what he was looking for.

The note, written in a scratchy hand, kept him focused on his goal. It reminded him that in spite of whatever enchantment Miss Cahill might possess on a stormy night, he would not be swayed by it during the full light of day.

He would face her, take what was his and be on his way.

Fifteen minutes later he stood at the front door of Leanna's Place. The paint on the sign over the entrance smelled fresh. She must have been at work before dawn. The sign hadn't been there last night.

Miss Cahill must be a hard worker. He tried not to admire her for that, but he fell a bit short. Hard work in anyone was an admirable quality.

"Leanna," he heard a woman's voice say from inside. The front door stood open but the voice came from a portion of the large room that he couldn't see. "Maybe we ought to wait on the postings another day so that we can get this place open on time."

"That would be the logical thing, Lucinda." Miss Cahill's voice hadn't lost a peck of charm by daylight. It carried out of the door as soft and melodious as he had feared. "But when I was here last night, I closed my eyes and listened. Those places across the tracks sounded every bit as wicked as the ones in Deadwood."

His task would be a lot easier if Leanna Cahill's voice didn't sound like a love song. Damn!

Cleve knocked on the doorframe. He stepped inside to find four women gathered about a table. Leanna sat with a pen in her hand; the other three stood behind her watching over her shoulder.

If Miss Cahill had looked fetching in trousers and a flannel shirt, she tripled the effect by wearing a dress. It was a practical gown of red gingham; nothing so special in that, except that it made her eyes blue as… What? Sky, bluebirds, blue birds' eggs?

"Mr. Holden!" She stood. Smaller hands than his could span that waistline. And the rest of what nature had given her, well, he wouldn't get a word out of his mouth if he looked at her chest a second longer. "How nice to see you again."

He had seen beautiful women before. In his line of work they came and went on a regular basis. As a gambler, he had encountered his share of scantily clad bosoms, but even with her dress buttoned to the neck, Miss Cahill's was more alluring than the lot of them put together.

She introduced her friends. Her employees, he discovered as the introductions went along. There was no hiding the fact that they were whores, in spite of the respectable clothing they wore at the moment.

It was their smiles that gave them away, something assessing in their glance. He'd been invited away from the card table by many such smiles, but he'd never accepted a single offer.

Each of those broken women had been someone's daughter…maybe someone's sister.

"Ladies," he said in response to the introductions. He removed his hat and turned it in his hands. "A pleasure."

All four women stared at him in silence for a moment.

Leanna spoke first. "All right, girls. When a gentleman greets a lady, she doesn't look at him like he's a dollar in the bank. Remember what we practiced."

Miss Cahill turned her attention on him. A clear blue lake is more what her eyes resembled. "May we borrow you for our lesson, Mr. Holden?"

"By all means." What was going on here? Was Miss Cahill teaching them advanced skills? How to entice a man with sophisticated ways?

He'd better state his business and in a hurry! The train was leaving in a couple of hours. Nothing would keep him from being on it.

The whore named Lucinda peered at him with her arms folded about her waist. She was a shade homely about the mouth but had black lustrous hair. She inclined her head an inch. "A pleasure, Mr. Holden," she said.

Cassie, a green-eyed beauty, straightened her back and copied what Lucinda did.

Massie, who looked too young and fresh even to be out of the schoolroom, presented a bobbing curtsy and a shy smile. "Pleasure, sir."

"No need to curtsy to a man, Massie," Miss Cahill advised. "A graceful acknowledgment of his presence will do. Like this."

Miss Cahill smiled brightly at him. She inclined her head a degree. She made a sweeping motion with her hand and pivoted slightly from the waist. "Welcome to Hearts for Harlots, Mr. Holden."

What kind of a name for a saloon was that? Not the one over the door.

The rumor about town was that Leanna's Place would be a den of iniquity that was sure to doom all of Cahill Crossing.

Beautiful beyond her reputation, a gifted card dealer who had made a fortune from her skills and her smiles, were just a few of the things that he had learned about her.

All reasons enough for him to be here.

"Hearts for Harlots?" he asked because he quite honestly couldn't think of an intelligent thing to say.

"Miss Leanna is teaching us proper ways," Massie said. "I'm hoping to be able to go home and see my folks. Maybe if they see a lady coming up the walk they'll think a minute before they toss me out."

He opened and closed his mouth like a gasping fish. Miss Cahill was running a sanctuary for unfortunate women?

"I wish you luck, Miss Monroe," he said when he recovered his voice. In fact, he couldn't think of anything he'd wished for more in a long while. "If I can be of any help…"

"Maybe you can take a glance at the handbill we are going to have printed," Lucinda said. "The sooner we get it passed around the dirty part of town, the sooner we can open Leanna's Place."

Miss Cahill picked the flyer up from the table and handed it to him. Her thumb brushed his in passing. The gash from last night's splinter was red but not swollen. Given a day or two it wouldn't pain her a bit.

He looked away from her slender fingers to the advertisement she had handed him.

The handbill invited any woman who wanted to change her life to come to Leanna's Place.

He was mightily confused. If he'd placed a wager on the purpose of this establishment he'd have lost every last cent. Miss Cahill must have read his puzzled expression.

"Leanna's Place is a gambling hall where gentlemen can come for entertainment that does not involve the purchase of a lady's favors," she explained.

"We are on a higher road now, Mr. Holden." Cassie smiled brightly at him. "Working here with Leanna to teach us respectable ways, we'll find the futures we've only dreamed of."

Everything that he'd believed of the scandalous Leanna Cahill had just been turned on its ear. That didn't mean he didn't have business to settle with her; it just made it a hell of a lot more difficult.

Taking something of value from a scandalous vixen would be easy; it would be right and decent.

Very clearly, Miss Cahill was not a scandalous vixen.

The back door flew open.

"Mama!" a young voice called. A boy, not more than a baby, really, careered across the floor and grasped Miss Cahill's skirt.

The memory of another baby's face flashed through his mind and he had to remind himself to breathe.

Leanna's child reached up his small sturdy arms. She caught him and spun him about, nuzzling her nose in his hair.

"There's my baby Boodle," she crooned into his neck. "I missed you so much."

All of a sudden the world felt off-kilter. Nothing that he had believed of the woman had been true, with the exception of her beauty.

"I kept him away as long as I could, Miss Leanna," a slender older woman said. Another whore, reforming, he supposed, looked him up and down. She seemed harder, more bitter than the others.

"He missed you something terrible so here we are."

"Thank you, Dorothy. I missed my baby something terrible, too."

The boy clung to Miss Cahill's neck, peeking out at him. Cleve resisted the urge to reach out and loop a whirl of fine dark hair about his thumb. Instead, he greeted Mrs. Wilmont, who had been introduced as Miss Cahill's housekeeper and nanny.

"He resembles you, Miss Cahill," Cleve admitted because, quite honestly, he did. He was a handsome child.

"He's got his uncle Bowie's blue eyes and his uncle Chance's temperament."

"Play," the boy said, or something like it.

Leanna let him down and he toddled toward the front door.

Cleve headed him off before he made it outside.

"You're a busy little man." He closed the door, then aimed him back toward Miss Cahill.

"Horsee!"

Miss Cahill stooped down to the boy's level. Her skirt billowed out and wrapped him up.

"All right, my little Boodle. I did promise you a horse ride."

"Boodle?" Cleve asked. What had the woman done, naming the child something so strange?

"It's a nickname." She stood with Boodle in her arms. He clasped his small arms about her neck and snuggled in. "His name is Cabe. *C* for Uncle Chance, *A* for…well, I needed a vowel to make sense of it. *B* for Uncle Bowie, *E* for Granddaddy Earl. His middle name is Quin for his uncle, my oldest brother."

No initial for his daddy, Cleve noted.

All at once the boy reached out his arms, clearly wanting Cleve to hold him. He thought he could, so he reached forward and Cabe Cahill came to him.

The ladies went back to work on the handbill. He listened to the drone of feminine voices while he chucked the boy under the chin and made him laugh.

Cabe was a very happy child.

"He likes you, Mr. Holden," Miss Cahill said, coming to stand beside them. She kissed young Boodle's pudgy hand. "He doesn't always take to strangers."

"I haven't always taken to babies, either. Looks like we'll get along just fine."

Miss Cahill laughed. Her eyes softened and he

was done. She was everything she had been last night and more.

"I reckon you've come to discuss that business from yesterday evening." She blinked at him with those lake-hued eyes and he nearly dropped little Cabe.

"Another time." He gave Cabe a squeeze, then handed him over to Leanna.

He could hardly set straight what needed straightening with his mind in a jumble over who this woman really was. She wasn't the seductress that the town said she was. Well, she was, but not in a tawdry way. She was a high-class lady who could make a man's heart leap with a mere smile.

Any woman who did what she was doing, trying to save those who couldn't save themselves, was an angel on earth.

The heavenly seductress was turning his resolve into mush.

He couldn't set forth a firm countenance when the only part of him growing firm had no business doing it.

Dammit, there was another train leaving Cahill Crossing at noon tomorrow.

The afternoon could not have been better suited to take her son on a horse ride. Leanna sat upon Fey's back with Cabe in the saddle in front of her.

Summer air warmed her cheeks. The fresh scent

of green things growing beside the creek and the twitter of little birds in the brush welcomed her.

In spite of everything, she was glad to be home. At any rate, she couldn't have raised her son in Deadwood much longer. It was a rough town and no place to bring up a child.

Besides, Cabe had uncles right here in Cahill Crossing, if they would only accept him.

A time of reckoning was coming. She was surprised that she hadn't been paid a visit by Quin or Bowie already. Or had they so washed their hands of her that they wouldn't even acknowledge her return? Had her brothers turned their backs on her for good? She'd find out soon enough.

"Let's go, Fey," she said to the horse. "I've got someplace special to show our boy."

Fey picked up her pace, prancing and seeming happy. The horse had traveled this path many times in the past and was clearly pleased to be back in familiar pastures.

Boodle laughed belly deep at the increased speed. Heaven help her if he turned out like his uncle Chance.

It wasn't long before they arrived at the edge of Cherokee Bluff. Leanna remained in the saddle with Cabe tucked in close to her.

"You see that, baby?" Far below, the land stretched away in rolling green hills as far as she could see. Trees grew on the banks of Triple Creek, their leaves twisting in the breeze and reflecting sunlight. "There's the 4C.

"Uncle Quin runs it now, all by himself." So many emotions jumbled around in her heart. Nostalgia, grief, guilt, joy…lots of joy. And just now the joy poked through. She didn't know this firsthand, but rumor had it that Quin had found his one and only.

Good for Quin, and Bowie, too. That was another happy rumor; Bowie had found his own true love, as well.

"I suppose you'll have to settle for uncles, Boodle. I can't imagine there will be a one-and-only for me. If there is, he'll be some sort of saint to overlook what I've become." She ruffled Cabe's hair, watching brown then blue highlights shine in the black. "That's all right. I've got my little man."

It *was* all right. There was not a soul on earth she could love more than Cabe, anyway.

A cloud passed in front of the sun, its shadow sliding over the land below.

"Look, way off there in the distance." Leanna pointed to the spot. "See that smoke? It's coming from the house that Grandpa Earl built."

And where he's buried in the little valley nearby, right beside Mama.

She could hardly believe she was here. She would be able to visit the graves whenever she wanted. During her time in Deadwood, her exile and what she considered to be her growing up from a spoiled girl to a woman, she had longed for this day a million times.

"We'll visit soon, Papa…Mama." Boodle wouldn't understand much of what she told him, but she spoke out loud, anyway.

A dust cloud rose from a corral near one of the barns on the 4C. Maybe it was Quin going about the business of keeping the ranch running.

She didn't tell Cabe what had happened the last time she'd seen her brother.

Growing up, there had never been a moment Quin hadn't watched out for her. As the oldest, he had decided it was his job. Many years back, she'd wandered too far from the house and gotten lost. He'd found her on the banks of Triple Creek well after dark. He hadn't scolded her, though. He'd bundled her in a blanket because it was October and turning cold, and taken her home to Mama, who had been crying her eyes out. Mama had scolded her.

Until that last day, until the fight, Quin had been there, always on her side.

Bowie had indulged her. If she wanted candy, the next time Bowie went to town, he delighted her on his return by letting her draw a peppermint stick from his coat pocket. If she was in a snit over some little thing, he coaxed her out of the mood with a tickle or a handful of flowers. In her mind, growing up, Bowie had wanted nothing more than to indulge her every whim. She had let him, of course.

Chance had never let her get away with anything, unless she was getting away with something he was involved in. He had never minded when she sneaked out at night after him. They'd watched shooting stars until dawn. When she begged him to teach her to ride astride, in secret so Mama and Papa wouldn't know, he'd been happy to do it. He hadn't been so happy about teaching her to shoot a gun because she'd caught on so quickly. Over time her aim had become nearly as good as his.

After the family split up, Chance had become a bounty hunter. She'd remained in touch with him, even seen him on occasion during her time in Deadwood.

He had been out collecting a bounty when Quin had sent the wire wanting them to come home. He wouldn't know that Mama and Papa had been murdered—she still couldn't wrap her mind around that thought—until he got the letter she'd left for him with her landlady in Deadwood.

He'd be home as soon as he got the news, surely he would. With all of them working together they would discover what had happened to Mama and Papa. It might take some convincing to make her brothers understand that she would not be left out of the search for the killers, that she was no longer the baby sister who had to stay home and be pampered.

Making them come around to her way of thinking would not be easy.

There had never been a time when her brothers hadn't watched out for her. Boys on neighboring ranches had thought long and hard before they came to call.

Why, just before the tragedy, Preston Van Slyck had started to court her. She had most definitely decided to refuse him. When he did not respect her decision, Quin, Bowie and Chance had run him off the 4C with a boot to his backside, one kick from each brother.

Over the past two years she had discovered that she could get by without her big brothers as champions, but she still well and truly missed them.

Upon her arrival in Deadwood two years ago, she had sent each of her brothers, even Quin, a telegram giving her location. She had warned them not to come for her or she would find an even more wicked place to live. Deadwood was perfection, she'd told them.

Of course, it hadn't been perfection. She'd had no money of her own, except what Chance had slipped into her saddlebag—praise heaven for that. Thank goodness Chance had also taught her poker and other useful card games.

At the time, she hadn't wanted his help. She'd thought she could make it on her own, easily.

All too soon she'd discovered what became of women who thought the same and found out differently. They became prostitutes. Bought, sold and forgotten by families who used to love them.

Had it not been for Chance, she might have been one of them. She might have been like Arden Honeybee. No one knew how close she had come to sharing her friend's fate.

Leanna had been lucky to be able to earn money, lots of money, dealing cards. She was pretty enough and knew how to charm men. Social grace was not a part of her past that she'd left behind.

Flirt and tease as she might, she knew that a trip upstairs with a gentleman was a trip to ruin.

She could never take back the hateful words she had shouted at her mother that last, horrible day, but she wouldn't dishonor her memory now.

Every day she tried to behave like the lady Mama had brought her up to be.

Because of her friendship with Arden Honeybee, Leanna learned that women were women, no matter what they did for a living. She wanted to give the girls who had made that trip upstairs a way out of the lives they had chosen.

And so, Hearts for Harlots had been born. She'd saved every tip she'd ever earned toward that cause.

"You were kind to everyone, Mama, no matter who they were," she said to the clear blue sky. "I really was paying attention growing up, even though it was probably hard to tell. I'm trying to be more like you. Although, and you've probably noticed, I still have a weakness for a pretty dress."

A bird chattered in a tree and it sounded like laughter.

"Let's head on home, Boodle. Time for your nap."
She lifted his face and leaned down to kiss his nose.
"From way up in heaven, Grandma is so proud of
you."

Chapter Three

Because Leanna Cahill was not coldhearted, selfish or dishonorable, not any of the things he had prejudged her to be, Cleve had lost sleep again last night.

Dammit if he hadn't risen from bed, lit the lamp and practiced shuffling cards. Cards were predictable when one knew how to play them. It was easy to be in control when all that was needed to fall into place were hearts, clubs, diamonds and spades.

Over time he had found that there was something about the muffled sound of the deck—aces sliding over jacks and queens mingling with kings—that soothed him.

Usually.

He'd left the hotel again this morning just after breakfast, knowing that the business he had with Miss Cahill could not wait any longer.

Neither would the noon train.

While he walked he tried to come up with a plan to bring up the business. Unfortunately, the only plan that his mind seemed capable of forming had to do with kissing Miss Cahill.

Pretty kissable lips haunted his nights and disturbed his days.

Cleve slammed his hand on top of his hat. Weather in this part of Texas was fickle. Today, the wind blew. He strode with his head down, leaning into a gust.

A woman walked several yards ahead of him carrying a bucket. Some rotten, awful stench from the pail blew back at him.

The woman stopped in front of Leanna's Place. She glanced left, then right. Had she looked behind her she would have seen Cleve stepping double time.

She hurried up Leanna's front steps. He dashed up after her and grabbed the bucket an instant before she would have dumped the disgusting contents on the porch.

"Let go of me you…you…cur!" the woman, dull of hair and dress, yelped.

"Your kind isn't welcome at Leanna's Place," he told her.

It might not be his place to stand up for Miss Cahill, but she was doing a good and honorable thing by helping the helpless. He couldn't make himself turn a blind eye and mind his own business.

"My…kind?" The woman blinked at him, not seeming to comprehend that the thing she had intended to do was wrong.

"A judgmental..." He smiled down at her. Anyone passing by might think they were in involved in friendly conversation. "Narrow-minded...shrew."

He closed her fingers around the handle of the stinky pail.

She huffed, puffed out her chest, then stomped down the stairs, the stench of her refuse trailing behind.

There were worse names he should have called her but just inside the open door a boy sat on the floor shooting marbles. The child couldn't be more than eight years old.

"Nice shot," Cleve said to him, striding through the doorway.

"Thanks, mister." He looked up, his face covered in freckles and hope. "I'm Melvin. Like to play?"

"Maybe later, son. Miss Cahill looks like she needs some help with that lamp."

"Miss Cahill needs help," she cried out. "And in a hurry!"

Miss Cahill stood on a bench trying to hook a large glass lamp onto a chain dangling from the ceiling. Her arms strained with the weight of the ruby-red globe.

Crystal bangles clinked together. She slowly tipped backward. Apparently, she wasn't going to let go of the lamp even if she ended up on the floor sitting in a heap of shattered glass.

Cleve sprinted forward for the second time that morning. He leaped upon the bench, caught her about her waist with one hand and rescued the lamp with the other.

"Mr. Holden," she said. "You have a knack for turning up at the right time."

"I aim to be of service." Most of the time, at least.

Not today, though. Today he would set matters straight between them. No more being swayed by her charm, her beauty and, there was no denying, her good heart.

First, though, he needed to take his hand off her. Curse it, she was firm and warm under his fingertips. It felt nice to have her weight leaning into his palm.

This was a mistake, but he drew her closer...just an inch...to breathe in the fresh, clean scent of her. She was like a summer storm when the earth begins to get wet.

She tipped her head and arched a brow at him; one slender hand pressed his chest, maybe in protest or maybe for balance. Since she made no move to step off the bench, he lingered just a bit to watch her cheeks blush the most charming shade of pink.

If Miss Cahill was a fallen woman he was still a sodbuster back in Nebraska.

"Lucky thing for me." She placed her free hand under the globe. "I paid a pretty price for this fancy piece."

He lifted the lamp, and she pushed it up. The movement shifted her left breast. He couldn't help but notice since it was only an inhalation from his chest. The heat of her sizzled through his coat and shirt.

A trance must have taken hold of him. She smiled and everything went away. If life went on beyond the two of them, toe-to-toe on the bench, he didn't notice much.

If it weren't for the boy playing marbles on the floor and the woman weeping in the corner, he might do the one thing sure to cause him grief. He would claim the kiss he had been thinking about and for that one moment he wouldn't be sorry.

But there was a woman weeping in the corner.

"I'll need to see to that," Miss Cahill murmured, but made no move do it.

"May I call you Leanna?" He was a fool. It would be much easier to confront Miss Cahill than Leanna.

"That would be lovely." Like her smile. "I'd like to call you Cleve."

"I'd like to hear it."

The wailing from the corner grew louder.

"I'll need to get down…Cleve."

He stepped off the bench first, making sure that both of his hands cupped her waist for the five seconds it took to lift her down. It might have taken only one second had a button on her dress not snagged a button of his coat.

Three seconds passed when she had to press into him in order to free herself.

At second number four, she pushed away but slowly, all the while looking into his eyes as though trying to see deeper than flesh would allow. He shouldn't want her to look so deeply but he watched her eyes the same way.

Both of them kept secrets.

Leanna turned all of a sudden. She hurried across the room.

"What is it, Massie?" She crouched down, eye to eye with the tearful dove who sat on the floor.

All of a sudden, the thought of breaking her heart made him feel hollow inside. For the first time he wondered if he was making a mistake.

"People hate us." Massie sniffed. "I'll never get to be respectable and go h-h-home."

"Of course you will!" Leanna stroked a lock of blond hair back from Massie's blotched face.

"But that awful woman was about to dump rotten potatoes on our porch. If Mr. Holden hadn't stopped her we'd have stunk to high heaven."

"Cleve? Did you do that?" Leanna blinked clear, dark-lashed eyes at him. Why did his name have to sound so special coming from her lips? He felt like a cad.

"Mr. Holden called her a shrew and sent her on her way, and her stinky bucket with her," young Melvin, still sitting on the floor with his marbles, declared. "I saw it all."

"Thank you, Cleve. That was kind of you."

"Anyone would have done the same." He'd do it again, a dozen times for Hearts for Harlots.

"Not around here, they wouldn't." Leanna helped

Massie to her feet, frowning. "I'm afraid you've cast your lot with us. When Mrs. Busybody spreads her righteous tale, your reputation won't be worth much."

"I'll be taking the train this noon. I won't be here long enough for it to matter."

He was a cad. He'd be gone, putting her firmly out of his mind, while she and the ladies dodged rotten potatoes.

"All the same, I'm sorry, Cleve."

She wouldn't be, though, once he told her what he had come for. He shouldn't feel guilty for doing the right thing. And he wouldn't if only she had been the woman her reputation claimed her to be.

Cleve wrestled with his conscience while Leanna sent Melvin home to play with Cabe, then gathered the ladies for a lesson.

If things were different, he'd pursue Leanna Cahill. Maybe even court her. He couldn't recall ever being so drawn to a woman. Forbidden fruit and all that, he reckoned.

"Cleve, will you act as our gentleman for this session?"

What he had come to do could wait half an hour. Who was he kidding? He knew he wouldn't be on that train.

He walked past the open front door and through a beam of sunlight. A leaf from the tree shading the front porch blew inside.

Leanna's students waited for him in the corner where Massie had been weeping.

"Ladies, always a pleasure," he said. Something inside him twisted, burned. If Leanna had been able to help his sister the way she was helping these ladies…well…life would be very different. He'd have no cause to be here now.

The sad fact was, she could not now be saved, but maybe these women could.

He would play their gentleman to the best of his ability, even though some would say he was no more a gentleman than Leanna was a lady.

"We practiced formal greetings yesterday, but I think we need a bit more work in that area," Leanna said. "First impressions are crucial. Lucinda, you go first. You are meeting Mr. Holden for the first time."

"Hello, mister." Lucinda arched her back and settled her shoulders. She rocked slightly side to side leading with her hips. Her dark gaze raked him, head to toe, then settled where it shouldn't.

"I think you got that all wrong, Lucinda," Cassie argued.

She tried the greeting herself but only succeeded in looking more a lady of the night than her friend.

"It's more like this," Leanna explained. "You stand an arm's length from the gentleman and extend your hand."

She demonstrated. Cleve took her hand and bowed just slightly over it. He didn't feel much like a gentleman, but he acted the part, anyway.

"You'll be wearing gloves during this greeting.

If you aren't, don't offer your hand. Just nod to acknowledge the gentleman."

Leanna withdrew her hand from his slowly, flesh to flesh with no annoying gloves to get in the way. Her skin was warm, smooth, and damned if he hadn't felt a spark kindle between their palms.

Well, then, she'd noticed it, too, if the sudden widening of her blue eyes meant anything.

"Like this?" Lucinda tried the nod.

"It's more subtle. You want to let the gent know you are interested, if you are. If you're not, we'll discuss how to handle that later. But in this instance, you do want him to know that you are, without him realizing that you know that you are."

"That sounds tricky, Miss Leanna," Cassie moaned.

"It is, a bit. Watch, I'll show you the difference."

Leanna swaggered up to him, her model. Her hips moved toward him with an exaggerated sway. Her breasts seemed to reach for him and her eyes, well, what was a man to say to that invitation?

She paced a slow circle around him, inhaling and taking his measure.

"Good evening," she purred.

A shadow blocked the light filtering through the doorway.

"Leanna Cahill, what the hell are you doing?" a voice thundered. "Mister, take a big step away!"

A man stomped into the room and, rather than wait for Cleve to step away, strode forward…arm swinging.

Leanna rushed between Cleve and the balled-up fist.

"Bowie!" She launched herself at the fellow and the swinging arm changed course to curl about her back.

The lawman, with his badge shining like a mirror, lifted Leanna off the floor and buried his face in the crook of her neck.

For half a heartbeat Cleve wanted to throttle him, as if he had any right to. Then he recalled the gossip. Leanna had three brothers, and one was a lawman.

This brother, Bowie, finally set her down and held her at arm's length, looking her over. "You okay?"

She nodded.

Apparently assured that she was hale and sound, he let his next emotion out.

"By hell, little sister, what was that?" He jerked his head toward Cleve, then slammed his hands on his gun belt, glaring at her. "I didn't believe what folks were saying. But here you are, bold as the devil, opening a hellhole, and on this side of the tracks! I ought to—"

"Hearts for Harlots," Cleve interrupted.

The marshal swung his angry gaze from his sister to Cleve. "Keep out of this, stranger."

"I would, but for some reason Miss Cahill seems too overcome to speak at the moment." And she did; her eyes were wet and her voice appeared to have dried up. She'd find it soon enough, he guessed.

Damned if Cleve would hold his tongue, though.

"Hearts for Harlots is a charity. Leanna's Place is not a brothel."

"Annie?" Bowie frowned at Leanna.

Quite honestly, Cleve was surprised that the man did not know his sister better than he did.

After being acquainted with Leanna for only a few days Cleve knew that there was not a dishonest bone in her. Well, there was…but only one.

"Fair gambling and some drinking is all that will be going on here," Cleve pointed out while Leanna managed a silent nod.

"That's not what it looked like when I walked in."

"Lesson in decorum." Cleve smiled at Lucinda, Cassie and Massie, who huddled together in the corner, apparently terrified of the glowering lawman. "For the employees. How to properly meet a respectable gentleman," he added in the face of Bowie Cahill's disbelief.

"Is this so, Annie?"

Cleve walked up to Leanna and stood beside her. He thought about clasping her hand in support, but brother Bowie's gun wasn't just for show.

"Why are you so determined to believe the gossip about your sister? These ladies—" Cleve indicated the fallen doves in the corner "—know the truth. Leanna has nothing to be ashamed of."

"I'm not determined to believe anything. I just want Annie to tell me herself what's going on."

Massie took two steps toward Marshal Cahill.

"Miss Leanna saved our lives," she declared. Cleve

wanted to applaud her show of courage. It couldn't have been easy for the former whore to stand up to a lawman.

Again, the twisting in his gut. If only Leanna had been able to save his sister. Maybe, though, no one could have. He sure hadn't been able to keep her from running away from home with some man who had promised the moon and then—

"I suppose Van Slyck was lying about a kid?" Marshal Cahill looked as if he wanted to believe it, but Leanna had paraded through town with the child on her lap.

That one would be tough.

"What about the boy? Is he yours?" her brother demanded.

Ah, there was the Leanna he had come to admire in such a short time. She flashed to life, glaring a dozen kinds of defiance at Bowie.

"Bone of my bone and flesh of my flesh," she admitted, her bearing that of a proud lioness. "His name is Cabe Cahill. Named after his uncles and Granddaddy Earl."

"Who's the father?" Bowie demanded.

Cleve presented a show of mild curiosity when in fact he wanted the answer to that question as badly as Bowie did.

"That is no one's business but mine." Leanna lifted up on her toes with her hands planted on her hips. She stared her brother down, glare for glare. "Don't ever ask me that again."

"Oh, hell, Annie." Bowie shook his head, dragging one hand down his face. "Quin's going to have a mouthful to say about you shaming the family name."

"If you ever utter the word *shame* with reference to my son again, Bowie Cahill, I'll slice up your tongue for dinner."

She would, too—maybe not literally, but he wouldn't want to be Bowie.

Hell, he didn't want to be himself.

There was something that only he and Leanna knew. It is what he had come to Cahill Crossing to set straight.

He reached into his pocket to touch his sister's letter.

The *A* in Cabe's name was not a fill-in letter. It stood for Arden.

Arden Holden, Cleve's late sister.

The woman who had given birth to Cabe.

Chapter Four

"Bowie." Leanna clasped her hands at her waist, breathing deep and forcing her temper to cool. "This is Cleve Holden. He's not the villain you mistook him for. I was simply giving the ladies an example of how not to act and Cleve was my model."

"I'll accept that for now," Bowie said. "But he looked too comfortable in his part, if you ask me."

"Well, I didn't ask you."

Leanna noticed Cleve glancing between her and Bowie with intense interest. Every now and again he opened his mouth, then closed it. His complexion looked flushed; frown lines sliced his forehead.

"A pleasure to meet you, Marshal Cahill," he said.

Unless she missed her guess, and she doubted that she had, Cleve's smile was forced.

Cleve extended his hand. Bowie looked him over,

head to toe and back again. Her brother grasped the offered palm.

"If Annie claims that you are upstanding, I'll accept that."

"I'll accept your distrust." The handshake ended. "I had a sister once."

Cleve's voice cracked on the word *once*. More than likely his sister had passed on.

Poor Cleve! She wanted to offer a comforting gesture but he stepped away.

"You and your brother must have some catching up to do." He nodded at her without a smile, then glanced toward the corner of the saloon. He tipped his hat. "Ladies."

He stepped out of the front door and down the stairs, bracing his hat against the wind. A whistle blew, announcing the arrival of the train.

Once again, Cleve had gone without discussing the business that had brought him to her in the first place. Since she didn't like wondering what it could be, she would make sure that next time nothing interfered with what he wanted to say.

Unless he had given up on the matter and was boarding the train. That had been his plan, after all. What on earth could he have wanted with her?

She might never see him again. That thought made her feel a bit gloomy. Surprised, too. Was it possible to pine for a man she had known such a brief time?

"Annie?" Bowie's voice called her back from staring at the empty doorway.

"Would you like to meet your nephew?" She rallied her wits back about her.

"It's not right that you won't say who he belongs to, Annie, but yes, I do want to meet him."

"He belongs to me. That's all you need to know." She tucked her hand into the crook of Bowie's arm. "Walk me home and we'll talk."

"Can't believe I'm an uncle. Does he look like me?"

He did, in fact, a little bit, with his dark hair and blue eyes. Cabe could easily pass for a Cahill to the casual observer.

If one looked close enough they might notice the small gold fleck in his left eye. It was in the shape of a half-moon with a star at the tip. It was subtle, impossible to see unless Cabe held still and you looked real close. Most folks would not even take note of it, but Cabe's father and grandfather had the identical marking.

She knew she had taken a risk bringing Cabe home. Both of those men lived in Cahill Crossing. Still, the odds were against either man paying a dot of attention to the baby—and Cabe never held still for long. Toddlers and grown men didn't travel in the same social circles.

Her little one was safe. If she didn't think so, she wouldn't have brought him here.

As much as she wanted to tell her brother who Cabe really was, that in fact she hadn't shamed the family with an illegitimate birth, she wouldn't. As a lawman, Bowie would feel bound to look for Cabe's mother's family, if there was one. They might be cheats, lairs and criminals for all she knew.

Her son might have a dozen relatives wanting him, and Leanna would fight each and every one of them. Cabe was hers in every way that really mattered.

Arden Honeybee, her dear friend from Deadwood, and a prostitute, had entrusted him to her care. It had been Arden's final wish for Leanna to raise her child, and to love it. During their short but close friendship, she had never mentioned a relative.

Arden's last breath had been Cabe's first. Leanna's ears had been the first to hear his newborn cry, her arms the first to hold him. She'd sobbed tears of grief and of welcome at the same time.

Arden had also entrusted her with a secret. The identity of her child's father. She had made Leanna vow never to reveal it.

Sometimes promises made on a death bed could be reconsidered later. This one could not.

Cabe's father was like opium, charming and seductive, and in the end the ruin of the most trusting of souls.

If he knew that sweet and lovely Arden had born him a son he might take him, turn him into someone like himself. Leanna would die before she let that happen.

As much as she wanted to reveal her secret to Bowie, she didn't dare. In spite of the fact that she had brought shame on the family, she knew that any one of her brothers would put themselves in harm's way to protect a nephew, a blood relative. She'd already lost Mama and Papa; she couldn't stand to lose a brother, too. Cabe's daddy was a warped man and he had warped friends.

Out on the street, summer wind blew hot against her back. It snapped the ends of the ribbon in her hair forward. She brushed the blue satin away from her mouth and held on to Bowie's arm while they walked past the general store. It felt good to lean into his strength for a moment.

Not longer than that, though. Two years had passed and she'd learned to rely on her own strength; she didn't want to give that up.

Just for this moment, though, she needed her brother. She rested her head on his arm.

He smiled down at her.

"That man is sweet on you," Bowie announced.

"Cleve?" She blinked at her brother, taken by surprise. "No, he isn't."

"I saw the way he looked before he figured I was your brother. He wasn't happy."

This was a silly conversation. What difference did it make if a man leaving town had feelings for her or not?

And in the end, she didn't want to spend this time with her brother discussing a flirtation.

She frowned, feeling the weight of what she had to discuss with Bowie settle upon her. She wanted to run away from it and not feel the pain, but it was there, always there.

"Murder? Truly?" She had trouble saying that awful word even though it replayed in her head time after time. "Couldn't that be a mistake?"

"It's not." Someone coming out of the general store sneered at her but retreated back inside when Bowie shot a fierce glare at him. "I'm sorry, Annie, the crash was staged to hide what really happened."

"Who would do that?" A lump swelled in her throat. She thought she was done with weeping, but maybe she never would be. "Why?"

"That's what we aim to find out." Bowie's jaw ticked. He clenched his fists. "Damned if I'll believe it's some Cahill Curse. Someone will answer for this."

Leanna stood away from him to wipe her face with both hands. She straightened her back and walked beside him.

"Tell me what I can do. This is what I came home for."

"I will, once I know."

"Promise me, Bowie." She grabbed his arm, squeezing tight. "I won't be left out of this."

"I promise." He covered her fingers with a return squeeze. "What about Chance, have you heard from him?"

"Not for a while. Bounty hunting keeps him busy and usually out of touch. Luckily, he was planning a visit to Deadwood when he finished the job he was on. I left a letter, and Quin's telegram, with my landlady. She'll make sure he gets it."

"You think she'll remember?"

"You can count on Mrs. Jameston—she is a dear. I used to bring harlots home to the boardinghouse, the ones who were trying to change their ways, and she never once looked down her nose at them, or me. But she is curious…and talkative. As sure as anything, she'll be watching out her window just waiting to give Chance the news. She'll try and console him, though, with a hug and a hot meal."

They turned right, walking past the church.

"Does Chance know who Cabe's pa is?"

She shook her head. "The last time I saw our brother he tried to force me to tell." She paused, and gave a short laugh. "I wonder how long it took that black eye to heal?"

They strolled past the school in the blessed shade of a cottonwood grove. A few hundred yards beyond that sat the house that Leanna had rented. It had a wide front porch that she would sit on one day when she had time. Trees growing on the east and west side blew in the wind. Leafy branches twisted their arms, waving a welcome.

"I hardly know you anymore, Annie." Bowie reached out to catch a leaf drifting down from a tree. "I can't figure you out. According to the town, you're a blight on the family name…. I wonder if you're the best one of us all."

"From what I hear, the Cahill Curse has claimed me."

The front door of Leanna's house opened. Dorothy walked outside with Cabe in her arms. She set him down.

"Mama!" Cabe raced toward her.

Her heart swelled watching his short legs pumping and his tiny boots stirring up a trail of dust.

"That's him?" Bowie crouched down at the same instant that Cabe slammed into her skirt. "I swear, Annie, I'll lay the man flat who says the boy is a curse."

Bowie reached out a finger to Cabe, but he leaned into flapping yards of blue calico and all but disappeared.

Bowie reached into his pocket. "Mind if I give him a peppermint stick? It always worked with you."

"You just happen to have one with you?"

"Just happen to."

Leanna was certain that mama was smiling down. Bowie didn't just happen to have candy in his pocket. He'd planned to accept his nephew all along.

I've got one of my brothers back, Mama, she said in her mind. *I might need some help with Quin, though.*

At sundown, the wind blew even harder. Trees cast long shifting shadows over the railroad tracks. Leaves skittered across the ground. They caught on the rails, twisted, shivered, then broke free and scurried toward town.

Leanna gathered the hem of her gown in the crook

of her elbow and hurried after them. She ought to have left the red-light part of town an hour earlier but a woman had clutched the flyer that Leanna had given her to her breast. She'd wept over it.

After spending an hour at the tawdry Hobart Hotel and Café, sipping stale coffee and nibbling staler pie, she'd convinced the woman to give Leanna's Place a try. The weary-looking prostitute promised to do it…as soon as she found the courage to leave her employer.

"Watch over that one if you can, Mama." Leanna stepped across the tracks, hugging the remaining flyers to her chest so they wouldn't blow away after the leaves. "It might not be safe for her once she walks away from that awful Hell's Corner Saloon. And she's so young, although she doesn't look it. Her name is Aggie."

Talking to Mama was something that Leanna couldn't quit doing. Just because Mama had passed over to the other side didn't mean she didn't hear what was going on in Leanna's mind. Some folks might laugh if they knew she did it. But she and her mother had been so close. What was between them couldn't have just gone away. The love existed somewhere.

The sun was dipping below the horizon by the time she walked between the train depot and the freight office. In a few minutes dusky shadows would give way to full dark.

A dog howled in the distance and someone yelled

at it. She quickened her pace. Being out alone after sundown in this part of town was an invitation to danger. At home, the ladies would begin to worry.

Behind her, the freight office and train depot stood dark and vacant. Before her, lights from the Château Royale flickered in the twilight.

Footsteps pounded the earth behind her, coming fast and heavy.

A light shone from a rear window of the telegraph office so she hurried that way.

The footsteps thudded beside her and then passed her. She stopped suddenly to avoid running into the man blocking her way.

"Preston." He looked down his straight and perfect nose at her, his smirk apparent in the flash of his white and perfect teeth. "You gave me a fright."

His snicker rustled the starched shirt beneath his evening coat.

"Forgive me. I wouldn't want to frighten Miss High-and-Mighty Cahill." He bent toward her, close enough that she smelled the cologne on his skin.

This was no cheap fragrance. For a bank clerk, he had expensive tastes.

"Not so high-and-mighty now, are you?" He caught a loose strand of her hair that blew toward him in the wind. He rubbed it between his thumb and fingers. "I'll bet you're good and sorry you turned me down, way back when. Who knows, you might be an honest woman right now if you hadn't."

It wouldn't do to make an enemy of Preston, at

least more than he already was, so she lifted her hair from his hand and tossed it back over her shoulder instead of slapping him.

"We never would have suited." She tried to step around him but he blocked her way.

"You damn Cahills." He propped one fist on his hip and arched a finely shaped eyebrow at her. "Damn you most of all. Still think you're better than everyone else? Even though folks snicker when you pass by?"

She would point out to him that the snickering was partly his fault. He was the one who had returned from Deadwood several months ago to gleefully spread the news that she was a mother with no wedding ring, but the less he thought about her child, the better. Besides, she *was* a mother with no wedding ring. She could hardly argue that.

"I don't want to keep you from your business across the tracks, Preston. No doubt the Fitzgerald boys are wondering what's keeping you."

"What they're wondering is what you are up to." He snatched the flyers from her and held them high in his pale, slender fingers. Wind snapped and nipped the paper. "Looks to me like you're trying to stir things up, deprive hardworking women of their livelihood."

While Preston deprived them of much more than that. She had never trusted him and, she had come to discover, with good cause.

He snickered again, deep down in his chest. He

opened his fist and let go of her flyers. They fluttered away like pale moths, tumbling and colliding in the dark.

"How ill-mannered of me!" He spread his hands wide, wiggled his fingers. "I do hope you will take offense, *Miss* Cahill."

"Grow up, Preston, before it's too late." She shook her head and took two steps around him, toward town.

He gripped her elbow and spun her back to face him.

"Don't dismiss me with your whiny little threat." He dug his fingers into her arm and shook her. "You pitiful whore!"

"Unless you want your face smashed in you'll let go of the lady," a voice spoke from behind her, its tone uncompromising. "Just to be clear, that was a threat."

Preston let go of her with a backward shove. She would have lost her balance but Cleve placed a steadying hand on her shoulder.

The fact that he hadn't left town relieved her nearly as much as seeing him in this very spot in the very instant that she needed an ally.

She glanced up at his face. Handsome, even when it looked set in stone, his expression spoke authority. He ordered Preston away like he was disciplining a disobedient dog.

Preston snorted. He brushed his coat with both hands. Stiff legged, he walked ten feet, then straightened his shoulders. Without a backward glance he strode toward Hell's Corner.

Hopefully, poor Aggie wouldn't be the one he took his anger out on tonight.

"Mercy me, you gave us all a fright!" Dorothy declared, standing prim and proper on Leanna's front porch. She folded her arms across her apron and frowned down at her and Cleve, each with one foot on the bottom step. "Staying across the tracks until well after dark. I can't think of what might have happened if Mr. Holden hadn't come to call and gone looking for you."

"I'm in your debt good and deep, Cleve." She glanced up to see him grinning.

The crease in his cheek lifted his smile and nearly made her miss the next step. He was beyond attractive in his white shirt with the sleeves rolled to his elbows and his jacket slung across his shoulder.

"A girl could get used to having a man like you around. I'm half-sorry you won't be staying in Cahill Crossing."

"Only half?"

All right, more than half, but she could hardly admit that when he had stated his intention of leaving.

Besides, he was a charmer and a flirt. No doubt he'd lost track of the number of women he'd enchanted over the years.

"Since you came to call and ended up having to

go in search of me, I believe I owe you dinner. Won't you stay?"

She hoped his answer would be yes. It had been forever since she'd truly enjoyed a man's company, and truth be told, she did enjoy this man's company.

"I'd be delighted," he answered.

"The two of you will have to eat alone. The rest of us supped an hour ago." Dorothy studied them for a moment, looking first at Leanna, then at Cleve. A ghost of a smile teased her lips, which for Dorothy amounted to an earsplitting grin. She opened the screen door and waved them inside. "I'll warm up some supper but you'll have to eat it out back. It's bedtime for the boys and I don't want any distractions."

It seemed that the boys were already distracted. Cabe darted across the front room with Melvin in pursuit, hooting, laughing and swinging an invisible rope.

Years peeled away and memories of playing roundup with Chance flashed in her memory.

Leanna scooped up her son an instant before he plowed into Dorothy on her way into the kitchen.

"Mama loves her Boodle." She buried her nose in his dark curls and breathed in the precious scent of him. Becoming his mother was the finest thing that had ever happened to her. Silently, prayerfully, she thanked Arden for the gift.

When she looked up she saw Cleve gazing at her with the most peculiar expression on his face.

"Say good-night to Mr. Holden, baby."

Cleve stepped forward and took Cabe's small hand in his big one. He shook it, kissed the chubby little knuckles. "Good night, little man."

Leanna would bet a silver coin that something about saying good-night to Boodle had moved Cleve. Maybe he had a child himself, or perhaps his sister had been a baby when he lost her.

"Would you like to carry him upstairs?"

He shook his head and let go of Cabe's hand. "Some other time. I'll meet you out back."

Curious. Judging by the tender look on Cleve's face, she'd have wagered his answer would have been yes.

Twenty minutes later, after she had sung Cabe his lullaby and tucked his worn and favorite blanket around him, she went downstairs to the kitchen.

Dorothy stood in front of the stove, scrubbing a spot of something from it.

"Well," Dorothy said, wiping her hands on her apron. "The girls and I are turning in early tonight."

She walked across the room, then paused in the doorway.

"We like that man."

Dorothy winked. She went up the stairs.

Leanna liked him, too, more than a little. But he wouldn't be around long enough for the gossips to sink their teeth into.

She stepped onto the back porch, grateful that the wind had, at last, settled to an easy breeze.

Cleve sat on a blanket with one leg bent and the other stretched out. He rested one elbow on his knee, seeming to appreciate the scene before him. It was lovely and soothing behind the house with a stream that flowed at the property's edge and the big, lush trees growing beside it.

He tipped his head, apparently listening to leaves scratching and whispering against one another. They had that in common. Wind-ruffled leaves was among her favorite sounds.

A pair of lanterns illuminated a golden circle around her guest. Soft light shimmered in his rich brown hair. It defined the muscles of his forearms where his sleeves were rolled up.

He must have heard the rustle of her skirt when she came down the stairs because he turned his head and smiled. That simple gesture warmed her. A smile was a simple thing, really. One didn't realize how precious that common act of friendliness was until it was taken away.

But quite honestly, there was no denying that Cleve's smile was anything but common. It made heat simmer low in her belly. It coiled and fluttered to her fingers and toes.

She most definitely liked Cleve Holden more than a little, for all the good it would do her.

"Your friend knows her way around the kitchen." Cleve moved over a foot to give her room to sit down. "This smells good."

"Mrs. Jameston, my landlady in Deadwood, taught Dorothy to cook."

"I was in Deadwood not long ago—that's a rough place for a woman. Can't quite picture you there." He picked up a fried chicken leg. "Gossip has it you worked a saloon. I'm not sure I believe that."

"Gossip has it right. I dealt cards and flirted with men."

"We're kindred spirits, then. I play cards, a gambler by calling. Not much for flirting with men, though."

She laughed, and Cleve smiled. It had been too long since she had spent a pleasant time with a handsome man.

"If the timing had been different we might have met earlier." He took a bite of chicken, chewed, then swallowed. "Tastes even better than it smells. Dorothy has a gift."

"It just goes to show." Leanna gestured with a fried wing. "If you give someone a hand, who knows what they might accomplish?"

Cleve rolled the clean chicken bone between his fingers; he stared at the red-and-gold weave of the blanket. For some reason, he sighed.

A silver moon hung in the sky like a cradle. Lightning bugs darted about, their small lights blinking here and there. Maybe tomorrow night she would let Cabe stay up late enough to see them.

"You're such a puzzle, Leanna." Cleve wiped his mouth on a cloth napkin, set the bone on top of it and leaned toward her. Lines creased his forehead. Clearly, he wanted to put the pieces in order.

"I'm just your common, grown-up-spoiled, destined-to-become-the-fodder-of-gossip girl…and I have a weakness for pretty clothes."

He laughed. The rumble came from deep in his chest. A shiver tightened her belly.

"That's what folks believe. I'd wager there's a lot more to you than that."

"Why did you come to Cahill Crossing, Cleve?" She crossed her arms over her bent knees, rested her head on top of them and glanced at him sideways. "I know you have some kind of business to discuss with me. It's time you did."

A lightning bug buzzed her face. Cleve brushed it off but his finger lingered near her skin long after the bug had flown away. She turned her head an inch. He traced the curve of her cheek. The only reason she didn't kiss that finger was because she'd be mighty embarrassed if he didn't feel the same attraction to her as she did to him.

"For a gentleman, you have rugged hands."

"For a fallen woman, you have a blush the prettiest shade of pink."

Leanna hopped up from the blanket. A blush! How humiliating. She kicked off her shoes and peeled down her stockings. "Even after dark the air's a blister. Let's cool our feet in the stream."

Cleve stepped into the water a moment after she did with his pant legs rolled to midcalf.

"If you're scandalized by a woman's bare feet you'd best look away." Not just bare feet but ankles and shins, as well. She kicked a spray of water at him. "I'm afraid that growing up with three older brothers dulled my social sensibilities."

He glanced at her feet and shrugged. "Too much importance is placed on social sensibilities."

He aimed a spray of water back at her.

"Oh, this feels good." She wiggled her toes over smooth, cold stones.

Cleve reached down. He cupped water in his palm. "Not as good as this."

He dribbled a few drops on his neck.

He flicked the rest on hers. His fingers glistened with moisture. He held her gaze for a moment, then touched her throat, smoothing liquid heat from her jawline to the hollow of her throat and up again. Cool water dripped down her neck. A single drop slipped between her breasts and tickled.

A firefly blinked between them. Its light flashed, reflecting in the earthy shimmer of his eyes.

His weight shifted toward her.

Cleve Holden intended to kiss her. His breath, warm and scented with their recent meal, skimmed her lips. Long seconds passed while he seemed to wait for her to accept the kiss or move away.

The decision would be hers.

A mere inch forward would give her what she longed for, to taste Cleve, and to feel him.

But at what cost?

He was leaving town, and very soon. What if every kiss she got from here to forever came up short?

She stepped away and Cleve let her. Half of her wished that he had pulled her back and into his arms, consumed her lips until she didn't care about tomorrow.

She walked south, nudging pebbles with her toes. He kept pace beside her, silent, with his hands shoved in his pockets.

Moonlight shivered in the current. Frogs croaked from the muddy bank.

"What is it about my little Cabe that draws you?" She stopped walking. Sand and water tickled her feet. "I see how you look at him. Do you have a child, or do you see your sister in him? Or maybe you want to tell me to mind my own business."

"Yes…and no. I don't have a child, and yes, I do see my sister in him."

"You don't want me to mind my own business?"

He shook his head, snatched her hand and led her along while they shuffled through the shallow stream. The gesture nearly brought her to tears. Folks touched hands all the time but his fingers twining through hers made her imagine that she was special to him.

Maybe she ought to have let him kiss her.

"Was she young, then, when she passed?"

"She was seventeen when she ran away from

home, but probably a hundred hard years old when she died," he murmured.

"Are you saying…?" She shook her head; now she was asking things that were too personal. "You don't need to talk about her if it's too painful."

"It is too painful, but I think you are the one person I ought to talk to."

They strolled through the water in silence. The battle inside him was plain to see. Keep his demons inside, or let her help him battle them.

"Our folks died when I was seventeen, my sister was fourteen," he said at last. "We didn't have any family to go to but we had the ranch that our folks left. I didn't know what else to do but keep the place going."

"Just like my oldest brother, Quin." She would ride out to the ranch soon. He probably didn't want to see her but he had a nephew to meet.

"It was a hard life, trying to do it on my own and raise a kid sister, but ranching is what I knew…what I loved."

She ached for Cleve.

She ached for Quin. It couldn't have been easy trying to keep Papa's dream alive all by himself.

"We got by for a couple of years, but little girls grow up. She took a fancy to a fellow passing through town. He was a real sweet-talker. He was no good and I told her so. She got angry with me. Said I couldn't judge someone I'd never even met. She ran off with him and I never saw her again. I got a letter from her, just once, saying that she was sorry…she was…she was in a tough situation. The— Sorry, any word that suits that man wouldn't be fit for your ears."

"Bastard?" she put in helpfully.

He nodded with his eyebrows disappearing under the hair that dipped over his forehead.

"Chance wasn't shy about what he said around me."

"All right, then. The bastard left my sister without a word and she was determined to make it on her own."

"I'm sorry, Cleve, truly. That's a common story and horrible every time. If only Hearts for Harlots could have helped her." He squeezed her hand. "What happened to the ranch?"

"Once my sister ran off, I lost the heart for it. I guessed the kind of work she would be doing so I took up gambling in the hopes that I'd come across her one day."

"It's not so difficult for a woman to disappear if she's set on not being found."

"I wish…" He stopped walking, gripped her shoulders, then pivoted her to face him. He lifted her chin. He did not mean to kiss her this time. While his expression was intense, it was not romantic. "You are doing a good thing, Leanna, with Hearts for Harlots."

"What was your sister's name? If she passed through Deadwood, I might remember her."

"That's what I came…" He stared into her eyes for a long time. He gazed so deeply that she thought he might see clear to her soul, to her secret. But then he shook his head.

"Tell me what's on your mind, Cleve."

"It's late...I've got to go."

And he did, just like that.

She watched him cross the yard in long strides, put on his shoes and disappear into the night.

Nothing would be gained by postponing, yet again, what needed to be done. This morning would be the last time Cleve would walk from the hotel to Leanna's Place without confronting her with the fact that he had come to take her son from her.

He would do it now or not at all. If he couldn't find the gumption to speak his mind, maybe he didn't deserve the boy.

Before stepping off the train in Cahill Crossing, he had been full of conviction. Right was right. That meant raising his sister's son.

It meant giving up the life of a gambler and buying a little ranch.

It meant settling down and finding the boy a suitable mother.

The hell of it was, Cabe already had a suitable mother who clearly loved him as much as Arden would have.

Heat pressed in on him as soon as he stepped off the porch of the Château Royale. He took off his coat and loosened his tie but it wasn't enough. Clouds hovered close to the earth, making the air thick and uncomfortable to breathe.

By the time he reached Leanna's Place he felt prickly with sweat and as edgy as a gambler on a losing streak.

The very last thing he wanted to do was break Leanna Cahill's heart. She was probably the finest woman he had ever met. She didn't deserve what he was about to do to her.

As far as that went, neither did innocent little Cabe. Losing the only mother he'd ever known might scar him. That thought made him stop. He started to turn around…to forget the whole thing and go back. But in the end, blood was blood. Arden would want him to raise her son.

A niggling voice in his head reminded him that, were that the case, she would have told him where she was. He wouldn't have had to sleuth about, searching town after town, tracking Arden's baby.

It struck him that perhaps his reasons for taking Cabe from Leanna might not be as noble as he told himself. In the end, was he just trying to get his sister back through the boy?

He stepped through the front door of Leanna's Place prepared to do what he had to, but not thinking much of himself for doing it.

The saloon was finally polished and shining. Carpets lay over gleaming wood floors, a piano sat beside a big fireplace that was filled with cut sunflowers. Bar stools, with cushions that matched the carpets, were placed before a long counter. A mirror on the mantelpiece reflected it from wall to wall. Poker tables took up most of the big room but there was space for dining tables near the piano and the fireplace. Chairs and couches had been scattered about the perimeter in arrangements that invited conversation.

Leanna's Place breathed elegance and welcome. The ladies ought to be proud of their hard work, smiling instead of sniffing and dabbing their eyes.

Lucinda wasn't sniffing, though. She paced from one end of the long room to the other, cursing Cahill Crossing and everyone in it.

Leanna stood near a window that faced the street, sweeping glass off the floor.

"Our new window will be here soon," she said, while shoving a shard of glass with the toe of her boot. "It's prettier than this one, anyway. It's a big stained-glass picture of a pasture and grazing horses."

"What's this?" Cleve must have bellowed because the women who hadn't noticed him enter jumped.

"Cleve!" Leanna leaned her broom against the wall and hurried toward him. She tugged the bow at the back of her apron, straightened it. She wiped her hands on the front. "It's good to see a friendly face."

"What happened here?"

"Someone threw a rock through our window," Lucinda spat. "A second sooner and it would have hit Miss Leanna."

Cleve closed his eyes. He sucked in a clammy breath. If Leanna chose to expose herself to ridicule for no good reason that he could figure out, that was her choice.

But physical danger? That was all the more reason to take his sister's child and get out of this town. A pretty little ranch seemed better by the moment.

Why couldn't he banish that nagging voice in his mind? It wasn't his fault that Leanna would be left brokenhearted in a place that reviled her.

Still, whatever decisions she'd made in her life had nothing to do with him. If those decisions put her in danger, he wasn't her brother or her husband...hell, he wasn't even her lover.

A man who had never even kissed a woman had no obligation to act as her protector. He had one obligation and he'd come to take care of that.

"Is there someplace we can talk privately?" He needed to settle this and in a hurry, before he got caught in the dewy blue glow of her eyes and ignored, once again, the reason he had come.

"I've only got a moment." She walked before him out of the back door, then closed it behind them. "I promised Cabe we'd spend the whole day together. Maybe you'd like to come riding with us?"

That careless thinking alone was reason for him to take the boy. Where was the woman's common sense? Riding alone after the threat she had just received?

"No, I—" All of a sudden his tongue wouldn't

work. It lay against the roof of his mouth thick as a wadded-up playing card. "It's time to settle that business I've been putting off."

"It's high time. I'm sure it can't possibly be as dour as the expression on your face."

She smiled at him and his heart shot straight to his gut. She had no idea that he was about to leave her bereft.

It would be easier if he didn't have to discuss it right here in the very spot he had first seen her weeping her heart out. He'd thought then that she looked like an angel.

It turned out that she was an angel…and a mystery.

What other woman would sacrifice her reputation to be a mother to an orphan and a friend to the fallen? He couldn't think of a single damn one.

"What is it, Cleve?"

She looked up at him with damp ringlets sticking to her forehead and temples. Sweat moistened her upper lip and glistened on her neck. Pink lace stretched across her bosom, rising and falling with her breathing.

"I've been meaning to speak with you…. There's something…I… It's about—"

Oh, hell and damn!

He wrapped both hands around her snip of a waist and lifted her. He drew her against his chest. Her breathing, quick and fast, matched his.

He kissed her deeply, thoroughly and, he feared, with his heart.

There! Now, he had the right to protect her.

He set her down and watched her eyes slowly open. It was like the sun rising on a bright clear morning. Like an old dream dying but a new one on the rise.

"I'm a gambler. I'm good at it." He let his hands linger on her waist because something about it felt right. "The thing I've been meaning to talk to you about is a job. I'd like you to hire me."

Chapter Five

Leanna sat alone at a poker table wearing her favorite gown. This pink dress of fine silk had earned her a bucket load of tips over the past couple of years. It was seductive enough to keep a gentleman's attention not wholly on his game while modest enough that he wasn't fully aware why.

She shuffled a deck of cards, then shuffled them again. It would be nice to blame the fact that she had only one customer on the persistent drizzle that had been falling all day, but the establishments on the other side of the tracks were as busy as fleas on a dog.

Her one patron, the young man who had delivered her goods from the train depot, was well into his fourth beer and a deep conversation with Massie. Even if the room were alive with gaiety and music he would be too smitten to notice.

At least Hearts for Harlots was a success. It was plain as a penny that Massie would soon be returning home with a husband and a bright, shiny ring to lead the way.

It was for the best, really, that the opening of Leanna's Place was off to a slow start. Her mind wasn't as sharp as it ought to be this evening.

It hadn't been for a couple of nights. The daytime hours passed easily enough, full of things to keep her mind focused. But when the sun set, so did sound thinking.

As soon as Cleve arrived for work, moths flipped about in her belly, the same as they battered the lamps hanging on the porch.

Every time he looked at her, and it was often, she felt his kiss warm her lips all over again.

The blush heating her cheeks was not the worldly image she sought to portray. How was she to play the part of a world-wise saloon keeper when it wasn't only her mouth growing warm when he glanced at her with a secret and a smile.

She really ought to stop reliving that kiss in her mind, nurturing and polishing it as though it were a gold nugget.

Cleve had wanted a job, and had been very persuasive in applying for it. She ought to leave what had happened between them as simply that. A simple kiss, a onetime kiss.

The man was a flirt to the bone, she understood that, and still she couldn't shake the feeling that there was quite a bit more to the kiss than "Won't you hire me?"

In case the kiss hadn't been enough to sway her, he had pointed out that Leanna's Place needed a man for the sake of the ladies. He would watch over them in ways she might not be able to.

He'd taken on the role of champion to her girls. Maybe that is what made her feel so tenderly toward him, that made her long to kiss him again.

Just now Cleve leaned against the frame of the open front door with his arms folded across his chest, gazing out at the drippy night. His black suit and white shirt indicated that he was ready for business. His necktie was knotted in a bow of the latest fashion and his boots reflected the light of the lanterns hanging on each side of the door.

He looked polished, suave, a professional gambler to the core.

She and Cleve were alike in some ways. They weren't fully what they appeared to be. How many women knew that beneath the natty clothing his muscles were firm and warm? How many knew that one of his kisses could melt the most tightly bound corset strings? How many guessed that the quick-fingered man of cards had an honest heart and that he cared for the plight of helpless women?

She didn't want to guess how many women knew those things, but *she* knew them and they touched her. Cleve Holden was quickly winning a piece of her heart.

Cleve straightened away from the door, then crossed the room. He pulled out a chair at her poker table and sat down.

"It's early," he said. "Things are bound to liven up."

"What do you think of the young man with Massie?"

Cleve plucked the cards from her fingers. He shot her the smile where one side of his mouth lifted slightly higher than the other and a pair of creases flashed in his cheek. "Let's draw high card to see who gets to have a word with him."

He shuffled the deck, then set the cards between them.

Leanna drew a jack of spades; Cleve claimed to have picked a queen of hearts.

"I'll catch him on his way out." Cleve shuffled again. "One more round?"

"What are we playing for?" She drew a card and left it facedown on the table.

"I draw high, you go riding with me."

"And if I drew high?"

"I go riding with you."

Leanna turned over the ace of clubs.

Somehow, Cleve pulled out the ace of diamonds.

"Imagine that?" he said with a lift of one brow.

"We go riding with each other," she answered with her mind full of visions of a day alone with Cleve.

"You have a lovely blush."

"I don't…" How could she? She had never been the blushing type before.

She wasn't able to argue against the telltale color in her cheeks because in that instant customers walked into the saloon.

Leanna stood. She tweaked the silk gathers of her skirt, then walked forward to welcome Willem Van Slyck, Cahill Crossing's banker.

From the corner of her eye she saw Lucinda and Cassie taking note of how the greeting was performed. Massie looked away from her young man with a sigh.

Leanna was more than half-surprised to see the banker. She had invited him last week when she'd opened the account for Leanna's Place, but to Van Slyck, social appearances meant a great deal.

The banker was tall, like his son, Preston. At one time he would have had Preston's good looks but the years had dimmed them. His graying hair, neatly trimmed along with his mustache and beard, announced his age, but it was the shadows and puffiness under his eyes that hinted of a soft, indulgent life. Still, his suit, precisely pressed, was the height of fashion.

The senior Van Slyck had been unmarried for as long as she could remember. There had been rumors of a wife who had run out on him. The story was, the woman had returned for the instant of time it took to leave the infant Preston on his doorstep.

Cleve shook the banker's hand and invited him to

a game of cards. Van Slyck declined, saying that he hadn't come to gamble but to spend a quiet evening in a place that wasn't tainted by loose women and dodgy dealings.

A few moments later, Lucas Burnett, the owner of a ranch that bordered the 4C, came in combing away raindrops from his black hair with his fingers. He nodded a greeting to her, then to Cleve. He strode toward the bar.

The next patron to come through the door was another neighbor of the 4C—Don Fitzgerald.

"Leanna?" He made to pat her shoulder like she was still the little girl who lived next door. Seeing her shoulder bare, he hesitated, then nodded his head instead. "Fine place. Good luck with it."

At the bar, Fitzgerald had a short conversation with Lucas Burnett. He shook Burnett's hand, took the drink he had ordered, then went to sit with Willem Van Slyck.

The rancher was a rugged-looking man, even in his evening clothes. He wore his mustache full and long enough to curl at the tips. He had sharp eyes that looked as though they had never crinkled in humor.

From his stool at the bar, Burnett watched his neighbor chat with the banker. He finished his drink and went out the front door.

An hour later Arthur Slocum, Cahill's longtime lawyer, joined Willem and Don.

Things were looking up. If men of their social standing spread the word that Leanna's Place was not a viper's nest, perhaps the wives of other respectable citizens would allow their husbands a night out.

Several customers came and went. The last three were not who she had hoped for.

Preston swaggered through the open door with a woman squeezed between his ribs and underarm. Ira and Johny Fitzgerald strolled in behind him. Like their fathers, Preston and the Fitzgerald boys seemed an unlikely alliance.

While Preston appeared as well-heeled as Willem, Ira and Johny looked as wild as a pair of tumbleweeds.

All three of them were trouble. Preston only looked more civilized, which, she supposed, made him all the more dangerous.

"Good evening, Father." It was early and already Preston's words were slightly slurred.

Willem shot his son a frown. "That woman doesn't belong here, Preston. If you want to stay you'll have to send her back."

Ira Fitzgerald bumped the girl with his hip and ogled her mostly exposed bosom with pale blue eyes.

"Aggie is the reason we're here." Preston slashed a handsome smile at the clearly frightened woman. "It seems that Miss Cahill has been troubling the ladies across the way. Filling their heads with hopes, dreams…lies. Isn't that right, Aggie?"

Johny Fitzgerald spun Aggie out from under Preston's arm. He pinched her breast.

"Whores only dream of men and money, isn't that right, Ag?"

"That's right, Johny." Aggie stared at the floor.

"Don't disgrace me, Preston. You're drunk." Willem scowled at his offspring.

"Just a little, Father. Never fear, we'll be on our way as soon as Miss Cahill hears what Aggie came to say."

"You mean what you dragged her here to say." Leanna was trying her best not to make an enemy of Preston, but poor Aggie was frightened. "Aggie, you don't have to leave with them."

"Say your piece, Ag." Johny patted her on the rear.

"Miss Cahill," she murmured. "I know you mean well, but we don't want you making trouble. I like what I do, the men and the money. Just stay away, that's what I came to say."

Flanked on one side by Preston, Johny on the other and Ira at her back, Aggie spun away and pushed through the men toward the door.

Her escape was blocked by Cleve, who filled the doorway, his legs braced. He caught her by the upper arms and stared down at her.

"Miss Aggie, don't go with them," he said in a low, firm voice. "You'll be safe here."

"I'm safe with the boys." Leanna saw Aggie's eyes glisten looking up at Cleve. "They take real good care of all the girls."

She wrenched out of Cleve's grip and dashed into the night. Preston, Johny and Ira followed, laughing.

"We've got us some wild sons, Willem," Don said, his voice carrying across the room. He twirled his mustache and propped his boots on a table.

"You proud of that?" Willem waved to Massie, ordering another drink. "I'll be relieved when Preston learns to act like a man."

"A man like you?" Don laughed low in his chest and swirled the whiskey in his glass.

The next morning, summer was at its most well behaved. Not too hot or windy or too extreme of anything, except beauty.

Weather-wise, it was a perfect day to go riding with Cleve, but a storm brewed in her belly.

The confrontation that she had dreaded for two years was coming upon her before she had emotionally prepared for it.

Bowie had informed her only an hour ago that Quin was leaving town to visit his new wife's estate in the East. If Leanna wanted to resolve her estrangement with her brother, it would have to be now.

For the better part of an hour poor Cleve rode beside her, probably wondering why she was so distracted.

In the end, she told him about Quin. How, growing up, he had been her protector, her champion against one and all, only to have their bond shattered on that horrible, miserable day of her parents' funeral.

Cleve admitted that he understood shattered bonds.

A short time later, crossing the yard of the home she had grown up in, her knees felt like jelly. Cleve walked close to her. It was silly, but it almost felt as if he had taken on the role that Quin had abandoned.

"Even though Mama is in the family plot, I see her everywhere, Cleve." She clasped his hand and felt his strength flow into her.

"When I left the homestead—" Cleve squeezed back "—I thought I saw my mother weeping. I can understand your brother wanting to hold it all together."

"I wonder if he still hates me."

"If you are Leanna Cahill, he never hated you."

Leanna and Cleve turned toward the voice coming from behind them.

A beautiful woman with pretty chestnut-colored hair and clear green eyes hurried forward wearing a stylish traveling gown. She kicked the skirt, then snagged the hem up in her fingers. She appeared annoyed that the pretty thing got in the way of her quick firm steps.

"You must be my sister-in-law," the woman said. "The rumors I've heard of your beauty are all true."

No doubt she'd heard many more rumors than that. Quin's wife must be a rare woman for not insulting her on the spot.

"I'm Leanna and this is Cleve Holden. You have to be Mrs. Cahill." Mama's name, she thought with an ache in her heart.

"Not to you, certainly." Mrs. Cahill's hug was

firm, her smile bright. "If you don't call me Addie K., I'll be distraught."

"I've come to visit my brother, Addie K., if he's willing to see me."

"Come inside." Addie K. preceded them up the front porch steps, clearly comfortable as lady of the house. "I'll have Elda bring you tea while I send Quin down."

She took three quick strides away, then turned and dashed back.

"Welcome home, Annie." She gave her another quick hug, then dashed up the stairs to the second story two at a time.

"There's Mama's bowl on the mantel." She walked forward and touched it. She took it down and pressed it to her heart. "Quin must have glued it back together."

"That's all I ever wanted, Annie," came Quin's voice from the top of the stairs. "To be the glue, to hold things together."

Leanna set the bowl carefully back in its place.

"We knew that, Quin. I loved you for it, but..."

"It's all right." Quin came down the steps showing no signs of the wound he had recently recovered from. "I was as wrong as anyone else."

Quin spoke all the right words, but he was distant, not the same brother she had known. But which one of them could honestly say they were the same?

Not Leanna by a far shot. She had come home an

unwed mother. Quin would have a hard time getting over that.

"You've grown up, Annie." He faced her, unsmiling, with his hands stiff at his sides. From four feet away she felt his pain.

"Not the way you had hoped, though."

"I shouldn't have kicked you out the way I did. Whatever awful things happened to you are my fault."

"Nothing awful happened to me."

"But you have—"

"One of the most perfect children the good Lord ever made." That would need setting straight from the get-go if she and her brother were to reconcile.

"His name is Cabe Quin," Cleve put in. Oddly, Leanna thought he sounded as proud and defensive of Cabe as she did. "After his uncles. I'm Cleve Holden, by the way."

Wasn't she the social ninny? With the high emotion of seeing her brother she had neglected to introduce Cleve.

"My employee and friend," she added, grateful that he didn't seem offended by her lapse in manners.

She hadn't noticed Addie K. come back down the stairs but she stood beside Quin, her love for him apparent.

Quin crossed the distance between them to shake Cleve's hand. He stood close enough that Leanna would be able to touch her brother if she reached out.

"The house looks different, but I still feel Mama

here and there." Her brother didn't move, unless you counted the welling moisture in his eyes. "I missed you every day, Quin."

Addie K. nudged Quin in the ribs with her elbow. He shot his wife a frown.

"He missed you, too," Addie K. stated. "He's just too stubborn to admit it."

"My wife, as always, is right and not afraid to let me know." Quin took Mama's bowl from the mantel. He placed it in her hands. "You keep this…forgive me, Annie."

With great care, she handed the bowl to Cleve.

"If you forgive me." She flung her arms around Quin's neck; he lifted her up and she wept silently on his shoulder.

An hour later Leanna rode away with Cleve while her brother and his wife waved them goodbye. She was beyond grateful that they wanted to meet Cabe the moment they returned from the East Coast.

Leanna felt lighter than she had in some time. Her son now had two uncles who would watch out for him.

Cleve breathed in a lungful of summer air, held it, savored it and let it go. Afternoon sunshine grazed his shirt. It warmed his skin clear to the bone.

He'd met another Cahill brother, this one as powerful a man as Bowie. The Cahills, he was coming to discover, were a tight family, in spite of their recent estrangement. Even had he followed through with his plan to take Cabe away, he realized now he'd have met with a good deal of resistance. Probably in the form of drawn weapons.

But he would have faced that threat in order to raise his nephew and honor Arden. The thing he could no longer face was breaking Leanna Cahill's heart…and Cabe's in the bargain.

He glanced at her riding beside him. She sat in the saddle with her back arched, her face lifted to the sky.

He would need to figure out another way to be in his nephew's life, to teach him things that a boy needed to know, to protect him from gossips and to avenge him the loss of his mother.

His job working at Leanna's Place gave him a good reason to stay close. Even more, watching over Leanna's doves made grieving his sister more bearable. In a small way it made sense of her loss, in that something meaningful might spring from tragedy.

He owed Leanna too much to heartlessly rip the boy from her arms.

Leanna sighed and he had to glance away to keep from rudely staring at the rise and fall of her chest. That particular vice was quickly becoming a habit.

Out of the blue an idea came to him. To be honest, it wasn't the blue. It was more likely out of the depths of his being that the plan came to him.

It was a good idea, one that might achieve his goal without anyone being hurt.

The odds of her agreeing to it were slim, but he

was a persistent fellow. The land had taught him that out of rock-hard soil came the most amazing abundance.

"The 4C reminds me of my ranch, but a whole lot bigger," he said. And more profitable. He had to admire Quin for being able to hold everything together when his life had fallen apart.

"There's something about the land," he added a moment later.

"It calls you home." Leanna pointed out the very feeling nibbling at his soul. He had never wanted to give up his little ranch, but fear for Arden had forced his hand.

"Every now and again." He gazed at the gentle slope of the earth with bluebonnets nodding their petals at the matching sky. "I feel like a tree that got chopped down and hauled away for this or that, but my roots stayed put where they were."

"That's almost poetic, Cleve. Are you as good a rancher as you are a gambler?"

"No. How about you?"

"My brothers did all the work. I just tagged along after them having fun. I've made money—quite a bit of it, really—dealing cards. You might guess, Quin isn't overly pleased by it," she said.

"Would you want to try ranching again one day?"

"I will, one day. I want that for Cabe."

So did he. Raising Cabe on a ranch had been his intention since the day he'd ridden away and left his land behind.

"You love that boy like he was your—" Cleve nipped his tongue. He'd come within a word of revealing that he was wise to her secret. "Your very own heart."

He'd nearly ruined everything with a single careless moment. He could never let her know who he was. She would see him for who he was—a deceiver. He would end up in a more difficult situation than he was now. Those brothers of hers would be tough in a fight.

"My little Boodle is all that and more."

That was no secret, but something else was.

"Why won't you tell who his daddy is?"

Raising Cabe was only one of the things he needed to do. He would not draw an easy breath until he made the man who had ruined Arden pay.

"Some things are better left unknown." Leanna dismounted Fey and led the horse to a pool of clear water several yards away. "When a woman makes a mistake, the child shouldn't have to pay the price of that."

Cleve slid off his horse. It followed Fey to the water.

He sat down beside Leanna in the shade of an aspen. Its leaves twisted and whispered against one another; they shimmered in the sunshine. Arrows of light shot through and glimmered in her hair.

"He's a good-for-nothing, I gather?" He forced his voice to be casual when he wanted to tear the man apart word by word. If he blurted out his anger, though, he might never discover who the bastard was.

"It doesn't matter."

"Think about that a minute. What if he decides he wants Cabe and tries to take him from you? It would matter then."

Pity the man who tried to take Cabe from the good and decent woman who loved him. That change of attitude would have stunned Cleve, even yesterday.

Life, he was quickly learning, had a way of shuffling a fellow's goals and dealing him a new hand.

"I'll tell you one thing about him, Cleve. And that's more than anyone else knows." Leanna leaned back against the tree bark and closed her eyes. Black lashes skimmed fair skin. "He doesn't even know he's Cabe's father. I didn't tell him."

"The boy is going to need a father."

Her eyes came open slowly. Her gaze rested on him. She was by far the most beautiful woman he had ever seen.

"You've met two of my brothers. The other one is every bit as devoted to family as Quin and Bowie are. He'll have all the fathers he needs."

"Those are uncles. They'll have children of their own one day. Cabe needs a pa who is all his."

"The next time you see a respectable man with respectable intentions coming toward me, point him out." Leanna drew her knees up to her chest and locked her arms about them. "I won't settle for anything less for my son."

Well, dammit, neither would he.

Cleve pounded his chest with his thumb.

"Marry me, Leanna. I'll treat you and Cabe with all the respect you need."

"What? Cleve, I can't marry you!"

He'd stunned her for sure. Her pretty mouth fell open. She blinked like a blue-eyed owl.

Maybe he ought to have worked up to the proposal, wooed her a bit.

Marriage, though, was the perfect solution to his problem.

It would be good for her, as well. As her husband he would be able to protect both Leanna and Cabe, day and night. It wasn't right, but there were those in town who did not wish Cabe's lovely mother well.

Leanna's reputation might take another slide if she married a gambler, but in the end how much worse could it get? As far as he could tell, the benefits would be greater than the cost.

One benefit to the marriage was obvious. Sharing a bed with Leanna Cahill would be... The thought distracted him so thoroughly that he nearly forgot the true purpose of his proposal.

"I'll be a good husband to you. I'll love your boy as my own flesh and blood."

"Why?" Leanna stood and brushed blades of dry grass off her skirt. "We've known each other barely more than a blink. Why would you settle for a ruined woman and her child when you ought to be looking for a family of your own?"

She paced around the trunk of the tree. After three revolutions she stopped to gaze down at him.

"You don't love me," she pointed out.

"That could change." He stood and backed her against the tree trunk. He twined his fingers in hers, then lifted her hands and kissed each one. "I admire you with all my heart. You are one of the finest women I have had the pleasure to meet."

"I have four very dear friends working for me who feel the same way."

"Not the same." With their fingers joined, he drew them behind her back and tugged her to him. Her heart beat against his ribs. He breathed in the scent of her flesh where it was tender, just between her ear and her jaw. He tasted it with a slow flick of his tongue.

She melted against him. He kissed her hard… ardently.

"There's this between us and you know it," he whispered in her ear.

She tipped her head so that the curve of her ear met his lips. Her hair tickled his nose with the echo of meadow flowers.

"I expect you've kissed a passel of woman this way. I'm far from the first to share this dalliance with you." She sighed and closed her eyes. "As lovely as it is."

"I'll admit, I've dallied with a few, but I've never proposed to one of them." He nipped her earlobe and she sighed.

"Here's the truth, Leanna." And it was. No matter what else might be lies, this was true. "There is something between us. You know I feel it, and I know you feel it."

"It's not enough." She sighed, but the protest was weak. He'd show her that she didn't mean it.

"Let me prove it."

"You can't prove a feeling." A bee buzzed about her hair and he blew it away.

"I'll wager that I can."

"A night's pay, then." Her wager came in quick, shallow breaths. "You win, you make double. I win, you work for free."

"Deal." While she sounded breathless he had all but choked on that one word.

He let go of her hands so that he could slide open three buttons at the collar of her dress. He cupped the back of her head in his palm, loosening neatly coiled curls and letting them slide between his fingertips. He pressed his lips to the hollow of her throat, tasted woman and velvet flesh.

A tremor skittered against his mouth.

"Did you feel that?" He figured that alone would prove is point.

"I did not." She blinked her eyes, wide and certain.

Well, then, she'd have to notice that he'd slid open the buttons of her gown to the waist. He trailed his fingers over the curve of her breasts where they swelled over the top of her corset.

"What about that?"

"I might have, just a little," she whispered with her eyes dipping shut.

His heart tripped. She liked pretty underthings. Ivory lace and satin ribbons parted under his fingertips.

"Marry me," he croaked because the sight of her full, pink-tipped breasts spilling out, bare to the dappled sunshine, stole his breath and nearly buckled his knees.

He longed to take them in his mouth, to taste and tug at the summer-berry flesh. But this was a wager, not a wedding night.

"You're trembling." Damn, so was he! "That proves my point."

When he looked up, he found that she had been watching him watch her. Their gazes held for a long time, then she turned around and began buttoning her dress.

"You're so damn beautiful, Leanna. This could be enough for a start."

"I'll double your wages for one night." She spoke firmly. But glancing over her shoulder, her eyes looked soft and languid. "That does not mean I will marry you."

She turned about, her clothing restored but the blush-colored cheeks as vivid as a moment ago.

"Tell me you'll consider it."

"I'm not the woman you want," she murmured, her voice no louder than the leaves rustling in the tree overhead. "I can't marry you."

"Maybe not today." He kissed her again because he wanted one that had nothing to do with proving a point and everything to do with the sweet seductive flavor of her. "But you will and then I'll do a whole lot more than look at you."

Chapter Six

Marry Cleve? What a completely ridiculous idea.

Leanna stared blankly at her reflection in the vanity mirror with her brush in one hand and a hank of tangled hair in the other. Crickets in the yard below chirruped out their nightly song. The melody washed through her open window sweeter sounding than she had ever noticed before.

His proposal flattered her; it tempted her, even.

But to stand before the preacher and say, "I do"? What a perfectly preposterous idea.

While Cleve was not precisely a stranger, she really had known him only a short time. The very last thing she should do is commit her life, and Cabe's, to him.

But he had won the bet. There was something between them. It was there in a word, or a glance... or in a kiss.

Even now, remembering the way he had gazed upon her breasts, naked to everything but the dappled shade, made them pucker, twist and ache to be touched.

Just in case the evening itself wasn't hot enough to tempt a person to run about naked, Cleve's declaration that he intended to marry her and "do a whole lot more than look" was about to blister the nightclothes right off her.

On any other night her shift, made of the softest cotton, grazed her body as gently as flower petals.

Not tonight, though. Tonight it shifted over her flesh like a gambler's sensitive fingers, touching here and dealing pleasure there.

Leanna set the brush down. She watched her reflection frown. Even if she did want to marry Cleve, she couldn't.

She was a virgin, for mercy's sake! Her secret wouldn't hold an hour after the wedding vows were recited.

Besides all that, she hadn't come home to get married. Finding out who murdered her parents must come before anything else. She couldn't consider a future without resolving the past.

A breeze filtered through the open window. She crossed the room and leaned her head out to watch the stars blink and blur in the heat.

"I miss you, Mama. Tell Papa I miss him, too, and that we will make whoever took you from us pay for what they did. You and Papa were—I mean, are—

even from way up there, the best parents anyone could have. I guess you know that Cleve has asked me to marry him? He doesn't love me—I reckon you know that, too. The thing is, you and Papa were in love from the first time you looked at each other. I know it's silly for me to hope for the same thing, being in my position. I can't marry Cleve, can I?"

A day and a half had passed since that intimate moment under the tree. It was a wonder that she'd gotten a single thing done. Dealing cards felt like dealing slabs of lead. Ordinarily smiles from ordinary men turned into Cleve's seductive grin. No matter what direction her thoughts took, they ended up of Cleve. She couldn't even give the stray dog at the back door a scrap of food without wondering what it would be like to have a man—Cleve, to be exact—to pet and feed morning and night.

Below her in the yard movement caught her eye. Walking between shadow and moonlight it came toward the house from the stream, revealing a slender womanly form. It was only Dorothy, cooling off in the heat.

"Why not?" Dorothy asked, looking up at the window. "Why can't you marry him?" Moon glow sharpened the angular lines of her face.

"You startled me!" Leanna paused to consider what answer to give. "We aren't in love, is why." Leanna rested her chin in her palms. "Is it any cooler down there?"

"Not a whit, unless you're sitting in the stream."

Which she clearly had been doing. Her flannel gown dripped water from the modest neck to the hem. "In my experience love and marriage don't necessarily go together, anyway. Life with Cleve Holden wouldn't be half-bad for you. And Cabe needs a father."

"If I married him," Leanna said in a loud whisper, "he'd find out I'm not Cabe's mother."

"And what would be so horrible about that?"

"He'll want to know who the father is."

"I don't know why you're so all fired set on keeping that secret. Your life would be a whole lot easier if folks knew you're not ruined."

"I promised Arden, and there was a good reason for it."

"May the poor lamb rest in peace." Dorothy twisted her hair, wringing a stream of water from it. "I'll give you the advice your mother would if she were here. Marry Cleve."

"I can't do that."

Dorothy shrugged, then disappeared from Leanna's line of view. The kitchen door opened, then closed with a click.

"Mama, would you tell me to marry a man who doesn't love me?" A star shot across the sky but Leanna wasn't sure if that meant yes or no.

Cleve would marry Leanna. Dashing up the back stairs of the saloon in an early-morning downpour, he set his mind to it.

It was true that the proposal had been impulsive,

but over the past couple of days he had resolved that it was the only course of action that would do.

If Leanna turned him down a dozen times he would propose a dozen and one times.

Walking through the back room, Cleve heard men's voices in the main saloon.

"Move it that way an inch, Marvin," a voice ordered. "No…back this way a little… Wait…too far! Too far! Balance the top or it's going over!"

"I've got two hands, is all!" came the agitated response. "Move back, Miss Cahill, you'll only be in the way."

Cleve rushed into the saloon in time to reach over Leanna's head and steady the brand-new stained-glass window an instant before it would have toppled over.

"Cleve!" He took the weight from her, helping the carpenters with the balance. "By now I shouldn't be surprised that you show up when I need you the most."

"I'm handy to have around." *Marry me* is what he meant.

The carpenters hammered several nails into place. The window held secure in its frame.

It was a piece of art as much as a window. Horses and cattle grazed on green meadows and in the distance smoke rose from the chimney of a home that looked very much like Quin Cahill's. Leanna must have paid a pretty price for the thing.

This morning Leanna had dressed for work in

men's pants and a striped cotton shirt. She crossed the big saloon, passed through the small room behind it and out to the back porch. He followed, admiring the stretch and pull of the worn denim covering her pretty, round backside.

"What are you doing here this early?" she asked without looking at him, her attention given to a stack of crates waiting to be unloaded.

"I've come to ask for your hand."

She spun about and braced her arms across her middle.

He got down on one knee. "Marry me, Leanna."

"Don't be silly, Cleve." She yanked on the shoulder of his shirt. "Get up before someone sees you."

"This is an honest proposal and I don't mind who sees it." He got up but only because he couldn't kiss her from the bent-knee position as he intended to.

She looked relieved until he put his hands on her waist and lifted her onto the stack of crates. Eye to eye, she had no place to look but at him.

"This reminds me of the first time we met, with the rain and you looking so appealing in those trousers."

"I had work to get done then, too."

"You were crying that night."

She glanced down briefly, then back up. "Well, I'm not now."

"Walk down the aisle with me and I'll do my best to see that you never cry again." A stray raindrop glistened in a curl at her temple. He looped the curl around his finger to rub the moisture away, then traced the curve of her cheek. "I'll do all of the chores—you can write that in the vows if you want."

"My recollection of what's written in those vows is that you will love me and only me. You don't love me, Cleve…and I don't love you."

He leaned forward. Heaven's mercy if she didn't meet him halfway. He kissed her tenderly, sweetly, but for a long time.

"You know plenty of good people marry with a lot less. Give me a chance." He kissed her again. This time there was nothing tender or sweet about it. Something ignited between his mouth and hers that went far deeper than a meeting of lips. "Marry me."

"Mama! Where's you?" Small footsteps tapped across the saloon floor, then through the back room.

Cleve lifted Leanna off the crates.

"Here comes the very reason I can't marry you," she said.

"Or the reason you ought to." He kissed her one more time, brisk and quick. "You might just as well say yes here and now."

"Don't use that smile on me, Cleve Holden." She scooped Cabe up and marched toward the saloon. She spun about in the doorway and scowled at him. "I know a snake charmer when I see one."

This coming marriage might be for convenience, but he was going to enjoy every moment of it.

* * *

The morning storm had blown out leaving behind a balmy wind and a sky that sparkled with stars. Leanna was pleased to see the saloon swelling with patrons. This would be her most successful night by far.

The regulars were all in attendance. Massie's young beau watched her move about the room, smiling and clearly as smitten as ever. Willem Van Slyck along with Don Fitzgerald sat in their customary chairs, drinking and talking. Glen Whitaker, Bowie's deputy, set down his money at the poker table. He wasn't one of her favorites, or even a regular customer, but a patron was a patron, after all.

Of course there was Cleve, dealing cards and looking more distracting than ever in his finely cut black suit and his stylishly knotted tie. Had it only been his clothes and easy smile that made him so appealing, she might not have glanced his way every ten minutes.

The trouble was, under the suit moved the hard, lean muscles of a rancher and beat the heart of man used to getting his way, be it herding a willful cow or urging a crop out of stubborn ground. Cleve was accustomed to getting what he wanted.

And he wanted her.

Just why, she had yet to understand. Cahill Crossing was full of pretty, respectable women he could choose from. Her dear friend Ellie would top that list, although her mother, Minnie, would probably faint dead away to have a gambler as a son-in-law.

Somehow, the picture that came to mind of Ellie and Cleve giving each other loving glances and tender touches made her heart squeeze.

She shook off that tug to her soul and sat down at a table to deal cards to five men who waited impatiently to begin a game of blackjack. Whoever Cleve married was none of her business. The fortunate woman he chose to spend his life with would not be her.

It was very likely that the only men in her life would be the ones she dealt cards to, so she smiled at them, congratulated them or consoled them and collected their generous tips.

Even with her attention so occupied it was difficult not to notice Cleve at the next table. Simply listening to the low tones of his voice conducting business made her imagine things that could not be hers.

Things that *could* be hers, an inner voice reminded her, if she would say yes to them. She wouldn't, of course…she couldn't. The problem of her sexual innocence was not one she could see her way around.

Truthfulness in a marriage was all important, even one that was not based on love. She could not go to her marriage bed a virgin…and a liar.

She could admit the truth to Cleve beforehand, but she wasn't certain she ought to. Even though she liked Cleve—more than liked him, truth be told—she didn't know if she could trust him with the secret that she had guarded, even from her brothers.

The hum of activity in the saloon fell quiet for a second and then started up again.

Leanna glanced up to see Bowie standing in the doorway. He crossed the room toward her with long strides and the sweet scent of the night-blooming jasmine that grew beside the front door clinging to his clothes.

He scanned the room while he walked, apparently weighing the patrons and their behavior to see if all was conducted in a legal manner.

Brother Bowie would find no fault with Leanna's Place. She and Cleve had been diligent about keeping the saloon respectable. In the event that a patron made a disrespectful move toward one of the ladies, Cleve escorted him outside with instructions not to return until his behavior was more considered. The card games were fair and the whiskey not watered. Her brother was welcome to look high and low, he would find no fault.

"Gentlemen," Bowie greeted the men at her table. "Good evening, Annie. I'd like a word when you have a moment?"

"Make yourself at home, big brother, just until I deal my gentlemen a couple more winning hands." She gave the men a wink, then smiled at her brother.

Between dealing hands she watched Bowie move about the room, stopping to chat with Glen Whitaker, then Doc Lewis.

When Bowie approached Cleve's poker table, Cleve stood and shook his hand. After Cleve sat down, Bowie strode over to chat with Willem Van Slyck and Don Fitzgerald.

Leanna stood and excused herself to the gentlemen at her table. Bowie met her halfway across the room.

"Looks like I won't be making any arrests here, Annie. You've done a fine job."

"I appreciate that, Marshal Cahill."

"Is there some place we can talk in private?"

"The back porch?" Leanna led the way.

Outside, summer air, soft and blossom-scented, touched her face. From across the tracks the muffled sounds of drunken revelry met her ears.

"Any luck winning over the ladies across the tracks?" Bowie asked.

"Not much yet." She sighed. "Do you know Aggie Holt?"

"She's a timid thing, brings to mind a scared mouse?"

"Aggie is scared. She wants to get away from that life." Leanna nodded her head toward the lights across the tracks. "But Preston and those Fitzgerald boys intimidate her."

"I need a favor of you, Annie." Looking down, Bowie tapped his boot toe against the porch rail. "It has to do with Ma and Pa."

Everything went still. The noise from the red-light district blurred to a distant hum. In spite of the warm evening her arms chilled with goose bumps.

"Do you know something?"

"Maybe." Bowie skimmed his hand down her arm, smoothing out the chill. "You recall Marshal Hobbs?"

"He's as much the talk of the town as I am, I suppose."

"Then you know that he's the one who shot Merritt's friend."

"And that he was killed by the same sniper who shot your Merritt. I'm happy about the two of you, by the way. From what I recall, she is lovely."

Bowie smiled. "She's quite a woman, Annie."

"Do you think that Hobbs knew something about Mama and Papa and that's why the sniper shot him?"

"That's likely, but it's something that Merritt's friend, Saul Bream, said before he died that's got me puzzled."

"Sure are a lot of people dying."

"The secrets surrounding what happened to Ma and Pa go pretty deep. Yeah, Annie, we've got people being silenced left and right and only one clue for all that."

"It's something, at least. What do you need me to do?"

"Just before Saul passed, he said that he had heard Hobbs mention Van Slyck. I don't know what that means, if anything at all, but I notice Willem is a customer of yours."

"Regular as sundown."

"Can you keep your ears open? Stay safe, mind

you, while you're doing it. I don't want you to take any risks."

The very last thing she wanted was to take risks around the Van Slycks.

Mama and Papa, though… Leanna bit her lip. They deserved justice.

"If the Van Slycks are connected, I'll find it out."

"Be careful, Annie. I don't know that they are. Who knows what Saul even meant by what he said."

"Deathbed confessions ought to carry some weight."

"That's what I think and that's why I'm asking you to listen in on Van Slyck." Bowie cupped her face in his hands, looking her hard in the eye. "I'm also asking that you don't do more than that. Just tell me if you hear anything unusual and I'll take over from there. You said you wanted to be involved, but it's dangerous, Annie."

"I'll be careful," she promised her brother.

What she promised herself was to stop at nothing to discover who had murdered her parents.

Standing in the shadow of the back room, Cleve had overheard enough of Leanna's conversation with her brother to make his gut fist up in a knot.

He hadn't been listening long enough to understand the why's and how's of things, just long enough to know that Leanna was to spy on Van Slyck for some reason and that she had promised not to put herself in danger.

Surely her brother knew better than to believe her.

It was more important now than ever to get Leanna to marry him. Whatever she did would have a direct impact on Cabe. Never mind that marriage between them would be good, protecting his nephew from whatever danger the Cahills might be involved in was what mattered.

He strode out of the shadows onto the back porch.

"Good evening, Marshal Cahill," he said.

"Holden." Bowie nodded his head.

Cleve stood beside Leanna. It was a bold move to make in front of her brother, but he circled his arm about her waist. He squeezed it.

"I'd like to ask for your sister's hand in marriage."

"What…you?" Leanna wriggled away. She rounded on him. "I told you I won't marry you!"

"When the time comes that you change your mind, I'd like to have your brother's consent."

"Sounds like a respectable idea to me," Bowie declared, grinning. "Honor binds me to warn you, Cleve, that you'll have your hands full."

"Keep out of this, Bowie." Leanna turned on her brother with a hiss.

"Can't rightly do that since I'm the one he was speaking to."

"As I've pointed out to Mr. Holden time and again, he doesn't love me…and I don't love him."

To that, Bowie tilted his head, and arched his brows. He hugged his sister, then walked down the back steps. His shoulders shook with the laughter he suppressed.

"Now that I have your brother's blessing, Miss Cahill, may I come calling tomorrow morning?" he asked with no little humor suppressed of his own.

"No, you may not!"

"I'll be along at nine sharp. We'll have a picnic in the country."

"Cleve! No," he heard her call as he walked back inside the saloon and took his place at the poker table.

Chapter Seven

The next morning at five minutes until nine Leanna sat on her front porch watching for Cleve. She didn't like being corralled into going with him, but if she didn't go he'd only pester her until she did.

The fact that she had spent the better part of an hour dressing, and in one of her most fetching gowns at that, did not mean that she was eager for this outing. It was simply her way of getting back at Cleve. At besting him.

Wouldn't it serve him right to see her at her best and then have her turn down his proposal...yet again?

Mother would point out that her reasoning was vain and childish, but Cleve had it coming for refusing to accept her decision.

No doubt he imagined this little excursion would be one where he kissed her. No doubt he meant to fondle her in some forbidden way in order to make her come around to his point of view.

What he didn't know was that she was bringing along protection against his charm. At this very moment Cabe and Melvin hopped up and down in anticipation of the picnic.

That would nip the flame of Mr. Cleve Holden's plans! The look of disappointment on his face would be worth all the extra trouble she had taken to look her best.

A moment later, Cleve pulled in front of the house driving a pretty rented buggy, its fringe swaying to the gait of the horse that pulled it.

The grin on his face when she announced that Cabe and Melvin were coming along was a big disappointment. The man did not seem a bit sorry to have the boys as chaperones.

She certainly would not give him a kiss today… probably not tomorrow, either.

The buggy ride passed with Cleve telling Melvin hing stories and Cabe babbling "fis" over and over n, even though he had no idea what "fis" was.

y as she might, she couldn't fault Cleve for his of a picnic area. It was a grassy spot only from a stream where, yes, fish were bound to ntiful. There were trees for shade and open a s for sun. Birds sang in the branches overhead w le grass bent and sighed on a gentle breeze.

If a couple were truly courting, love would find a way this perfect, peaceful day.

Love, in fact, did seem to be blooming. Cabe and Melvin couldn't get enough of their new hero, Cleve. With lunch eaten and out of the way the boys were free to play. Horseback rides, and piggyback rides, hide-and-seek and tag were only warm-ups to fishing.

Cleve wouldn't know it, but his clear enjoyment of being with the boys had ruined her hard-won resentment of his high-handed behavior of last night.

Still, she would not kiss him, on that she remained firm.

Sitting on a quilt with her back against a tree trunk, she watched Cleve give each of the boys a fishing rod that he had fashioned from willow reeds. Strings tied to the ends of the reeds dangled in the water.

Melvin looked intent on listening to the instructions Cleve was giving on how to catch a fish. Cabe industriously clutched his willow pole in his fist and jabbered at it.

Cleve sat down on the stream bank with Melvin beside him and Cabe between his bent knees. No one caught a fish but that didn't seem to ruin any of the fun.

After a while Cabe drifted to sleep and dropped his mangled pole in the water. Cleve carried him back to the quilt and sat down beside her, shoulder to shoulder. He cradled Cabe close to his chest.

"I'll take him." She reached over but Cleve shook his head.

"If you don't mind, I'd like to hold him."

Surprisingly, she didn't mind. She supposed she ought to. It might not be wise for Cleve to form bonds with her Boodle. When the day came that he moved on, she didn't want her son's heart broken.

If she married him, though, he wouldn't move on. The sneaky thought poked at her mind, disturbing in its seduction.

"You're good with children." It was only fair to admit the truth.

"I used to be one."

"Everyone used to be one." But there was something about the way Cleve looked at her son. There was tenderness in the way he stroked the dark, sweat-dampened hair from Boodle's forehead.

Leanna glanced toward the stream to check on Melvin. He sat with his bare toes in the water and the fishing pole gripped in both fists.

"Is there even a hook on that line?" she asked.

"The bait's just tied to it." Cleve grinned at her. "Today we're fishing for nibbles."

Leanna closed her eyes, listening to the rush of the stream and the whisper of the grass. Just above her a bird hopped from branch to branch, twittering. Kisses of sunshine and shade crossed her face. Some moments should never end.

"What is it that your brother has you fishing for?"

Her lovely moment ended like a bucket of rainwater poured over her head.

"You spied on us last night?"

"Not on purpose, and I didn't hear it all, but enough to know that you could be in danger."

How, she wondered, did one accidentally spy on someone? She didn't ask because there was no point in casting a shadow on a lovely day.

"If you heard that," she said, sweet as sugar and spice, "then you know that I promised my brother that I would be careful."

"You think that Bowie walked away believing that promise?"

"Maybe not. Thanks to you he walked away believing I was about to become an honest woman."

Cleve adjusted Cabe in his arms. He sniffed her son's hair and kissed his round baby cheek, something a real father would do.

At that second Melvin jumped up. "I got a nibble, Mr. Holden! I got one!"

"Good work, son. Tie on more bait. See if you can get another."

"Yes, sir!" Melvin sat down and stuck his feet back in the water.

"Leanna, I've heard the rumors. Won't you tell me what really happened to your folks?"

"We're cursed, the whole lot of us. Ma and Pa killed, Quin nearly. And I've brought unbearable shame on the family by becoming a mother without a wedding ring."

"It is a tragedy about your folks. It was a blessing that Quin wasn't killed. This little fellow—" Cleve gazed down and smiled at the peaceful sleeping face "—is a miracle. As I see it, there is no curse."

Had Cleve kissed and wooed her for hours on end he could not have pressed his suit better. For just an instant she wondered if it might be possible to marry him.

It wouldn't, she knew that, but what if…

"Tell me your secrets, Leanna." He touched the hand that she had unthinkingly balled into a fist. "Let me help."

His fingers, warm and strong, stroked her knuckles. She didn't mean to, but she relaxed. Somehow, her head ended up leaning on his shoulder without her noticing it happen. Maybe he leaned in, maybe she did, but neither of them leaned away.

"My parents were coming home from Elk Grove when they died. I'm sure you know that from the gossip."

Cleve nodded; he nuzzled the top of her head with his cheek. Suddenly the whole awful story poured from her. She told him about the shock of the news and the horror of seeing her parents' bodies in the morgue in Elk Grove.

Moisture dampened her cheeks while she told him about the fight that had split the family for two years and how they were all coming back since Quin had discovered that their parents had been murdered. All but Chance, who would be along as soon as he got the news.

She wiped her cheeks dry. "Seems like I never

run out of tears. Anyway, lately, anyone who might know something about what happened ends up dead. The last fellow, Saul Bream, a friend of Bowie's girl, Merritt, lingered long enough to mention a name."

"Van Slyck," Cleve said. "I heard your brother say that."

"Bowie wants me to listen in on Willem, since he comes to our place regularly."

"And that's all you'll do?"

"Of course," she said.

He tipped his head back, peering closely at her face.

"There's no need to frown like that."

"I wouldn't if I believed you." His expression only deepened. "Anything besides listening you leave to me."

"You're my employee, Cleve. I won't ask you to be involved in my family's troubles."

"You can't leave me out of them, either. Just as soon as you marry me they will be my troubles, too."

"You know very well I'm not going to marry you." She wasn't going to kiss him, either, but before her head could object…she leaned over and did.

She wished she hadn't sighed out loud. If only she could taste Cleve without her heart going into a flutter.

A woman ought to be able to appreciate the flavor of a man without succumbing to him.

But there were fluttery wings tickling her heart and she hadn't a clue what to do about them.

"Many marriages start with less than this," Cleve murmured.

"I shouldn't marry you, Cleve." The sigh of hesitation in her voice wouldn't have happened had Boodle not stirred in his sleep, reached up a chubby hand and touched Cleve's nose.

"Fis," the sleepy young voice mumbled.

When Cleve kissed the chubby fist near his lips, it was as though he kissed her, too.

It would take more willpower than she had not to succumb to that tender seduction.

Leanna stared at the moon-bright night through the saloon's new stained-glass window. She didn't see much but Cleve's reflection in it, sitting at his table and dealing cards.

He spoke to his lone customer. Given that she stared at a reflected image, she was able to watch his lips grin, twitch in suppressed humor, then narrow in concentration, for quite some time without anyone knowing what she was about.

She couldn't recall ever seeing a man with a more appealing mouth.

She didn't want to, but she did like kissing Cleve. Three nights after the picnic she still daydreamed of the way he had captivated her after her last denial of his proposal.

He'd set Cabe down on the grass, glanced at Melvin, who had fallen asleep, pole in hand beside the stream, then turned his complete attention on her.

His first move of seduction had been with his eyes. Before his lips ever touched hers he'd looked at her long and hard. Long enough that he must have sensed that her refusal was not as firm as it had first been.

The kiss was different than any that had come before. Not playful or provocative, this one was intensely possessive. She would be his, it said, and nothing that she could do or say would change that.

He was a huntsman, and she his prey. He was pursuit and she…surrender.

The heat of her response, the way her bones melted to goopy mush, was impossible to deny. The grin he shot her when she finally managed to open her heavy lids told her that he had noticed.

What, she wondered while she tapped one finger on the glass, became of marriages that were based upon pleasures of the flesh? Maybe she ought to consider—

"Miss Cahill?"

"Yes, Mr. Webber?" Leanna said, spinning about with her cheeks flaming to face Massie's beau.

"I've brought a note for you from Miss Aggie."

He handed her a piece of paper that looked worn from repeated folding.

"I just want you to know that I wasn't over there for any wrong reason. I'm a changed man, thanks to Miss Massie."

"I'm pleased to hear that." She opened the note. "How did Miss Aggie seem?"

"Scared, I reckon. Sick, too." Massie's beau looked

at the floor. He scuffed his toe against the wood. "I used to be one of her regular customers, before Massie, that is. Aggie always did seem a timid thing, but now, well, I couldn't help but read what she wrote. She needs help, Miss Cahill, and in a hurry."

Leanna scanned the note. Sick and frightened summed it up.

"Thank you, Mr. Webber," she said before she hurried toward Cleve, dealing cards to a trio of men.

"Mr. Holden," she said. "May I have a word with you?"

"Of course, Miss Cahill." Cleve stood and waved his hand at Lucinda, the signal that a change in dealers was needed.

Leanna hurried ahead of Cleve toward the back porch. Striding close behind her, he shut the back door.

"I need your help, Cleve." She handed him the note. "You remember Aggie? She's ready to come to Leanna's Place but I think she is in danger."

"I'll go get her."

"Not without me."

"I'd argue that, if we had more time."

"I think I might love you." Leanna stood on her toes and hugged his neck.

She might love Cleve. She'd uttered that casually... in jest, but once said, the words hit her as the truth.

There was no time to dwell on that right now. She'd consider the startling consequences of that notion later.

Cleve snatched her hand. He kissed her knuckles, then kept hold of her while they ran out the back door toward the railroad tracks.

Cleve gripped Leanna's hand, setting a fast pace. At the outset, he'd worried that her silk skirt and dainty shoes might slow her down.

He needn't have been concerned. With her fancy hem tucked into the crook of her arm she skimmed the distance between the tracks and the bad part of town at the pace he set.

She looked like an angel doing it, too. Moonlight glinted in her dark hair and reflected in the gold threads of her dress. He imagined trumpets announcing her advance on Hell's Corner Saloon.

He wouldn't want to be the fellow who tried to keep her from retrieving Aggie.

"It's that last place on the end." Leanna stopped to catch her breath.

She pointed to a run-down-looking building. Lanterns with red glass hung from the eves of the porch, sending an odd glow onto the road. The open front doors spilled noise into the night and masked the natural sounds of crickets and frogs. A drunk stumbled outside, glanced at them, then undid his trousers to urinate where he stood.

Cleve nearly vomited. Had his sister worked in a place like this? Had she served such a man? He'd make sure Aggie made it out of here if it cost him his last breath. He hadn't been able to save his sister, but maybe this woman would get a second chance.

"It goes against the grain, not to go bursting inside and carry Aggie away in front of their noses," he grumbled. "But I reckon we ought to go about it more quietly."

Leanna nodded. "Aggie's note said she is on the second floor, the corner window around the back. Maybe there's a back stairwell."

There *was* a back stairwell. As luck would have it, the alley door leading to it stood open. The door swayed back and forth in the breeze, squealing on its hinges.

"Stay behind me," he whispered.

In the deep shadow of the hall he felt her fingers burrow into his coat sleeve.

Five steps down the hallway, he stopped abruptly. A voice carried from behind a half-closed door to the right.

"Preston," Leanna mouthed close to his ear. He frowned, recognizing that voice. The pair of times he'd encountered the man was a pair too many.

"Look here, Van Slyck," another voice said. "You're here to collect protection money? Well, I say, do some protecting."

"You are still in business," Preston's voice said with its usual arrogance.

"No thanks to the Cahill woman, putting ideas into the whores' heads. If Aggie wasn't locked in her room, she'd light out on me in a second, and some of the others with her. I make most of my money off the whores."

"Make an example of her."

Cleve felt Leanna's quick intake of breath.

"I beat her yesterday," the voice said. "I do it again too soon and she won't do me any good. The customers don't take to sickly women."

Leanna nodded, apparently agreeing with the curse he'd just blistered her ear with.

"Something's got to be done about that woman, Van Slyck."

"Don't forget who her brother is. You want to draw the attention of Marshal Cahill?"

"What about that kid of hers? That would be her weak spot, sure."

Leanna lurched toward the room but he restrained her. It was only concern for her safety that kept him from smashing the door wide and pounding the speaker to the floor.

"You are one evil bastard. The kid is just a baby," Preston said, but he laughed.

Cleve nodded his head toward the swinging back door, grateful that the squeal of the hinges covered the sound of their footsteps.

Once outside, he spun Leanna about to face him, gripping her upper arms. "Marry me or don't. Either way, I won't let anything happen to your son."

"I believe that, Cleve." He felt the tremor of anger running through her body. "Let's hurry and get Aggie out of here."

He scanned the back of the building. It was a flat surface with no upstairs porch to allow easy access to Aggie's room.

"There's only one way to get in there," Leanna whispered. "I'll stand on your shoulders, get inside, then hand her down to you."

"Too risky." He took her chin in his fingers and stared hard at her. "I won't have you up there alone."

"When I asked for your help I didn't put you in charge."

"Back at the saloon, you are in charge. I'll do every damn thing you tell me to. Right now you'll do what I say."

"Well, then, what do you say?" She glanced about as though daring him to find a way up to the room.

"There's a ladder over there behind the café." He pointed to where it lay in a trash pile not fifty feet away. "Wait here."

He returned a moment later with a ladder tall enough to reach the window but he wasn't certain it would hold his weight, let alone Aggie's, on the trip down. He set the spindly thing in front of the window and climbed up.

He felt the ladder's balance shift with the weight of Leanna coming up behind. He didn't have time to warn her to get down and it wouldn't have done any good, anyway. He needed to get Aggie away from here before someone decided to check on her, or before a client who didn't care that she was bruised and battered paid for her.

He reached the window. He tried to shove it up.

"Damn," he muttered.

"What is it?" Leanna asked from near his knee.

"Window's nailed in place." He glanced down. "There's an opening but it's too small for me to get through."

"I can get in." She shimmied up beside him, then squeezed through the crack.

Hell. He'd have held her back instead of helping her through had he not gotten a glimpse of the woman on the bed.

Feeling as useless as a bet against four aces, Cleve kept watch through the window.

Aggie lay on a stained mattress with her knees drawn to her chin, shivering in nothing but a thin, worn shift. Her shoulder looked purple, swelling where it must have been punched. Her cheek looked worse.

When Leanna touched her she recoiled with her fists in front of her face. A trickle of blood dripped from her lip.

"It's Leanna Cahill, Aggie." Leanna bent beside the bed, speaking in soft tones. "Mr. Holden and I have come for you."

"Oh, no. It isn't safe." She sat up with a groan. "You've got to go before he hears you."

"Can you make it to the window? Mr. Holden will carry you the rest of the way."

"What's going on in there, Aggie?" a voice said from the far side of the door. "Who you talking to?"

"To myself, is all." Leanna helped Aggie to her feet, with an arm around her waist to hold her upright. Too slowly, Aggie limped toward the window. "Just like before."

"Your papa ain't comin'. Might as well quit your blubberin'." Floorboards creaked as though the man had stood up from a chair. "I don't believe you're talking to your dead daddy, no how. Now, where'd I put them keys?"

Heavy footsteps thumped down the hall, growing fainter as the man neared the stairs that would lead down to the saloon.

"Come on, Aggie," Cleve said, reaching for her and easing her out of the window slot. "I've got you now."

"Hurry! I hear the guard coming back." Leanna eased out of the opening bottom first with her legs dangling out of the window. She scrambled backward but her skirt caught on a splinter. She tugged hard but the splinter held to the silk like it was stitched. "He's turning the key in the lock! Get Aggie out of here!"

Get Aggie out of here? Hell would bloom spring flowers before he'd leave Leanna to the guard.

He scrambled down the ladder, two rungs at a time, then set Aggie on the ground.

"Well, now, what do we have here?" He heard the guard laugh in a disgusting way. "Miss Aggie's replacement?"

Racing back up the ladder, the second rung

cracked under his boot. He made a leap. The forth rung held.

He reached the window in time to punch the guard in the face. He yanked Leanna's skirt free while the man ran bellowing down the hall, sounding an alarm.

In the seconds it took to get down the ladder and gather up Leanna and Aggie, the alley door flew open and Preston dashed out.

"You've got no right to abduct that woman." He strode forward with a self-assured gait. "She and the owner of this establishment have a contract."

Was it a contract that had kept Arden from coming home?

He set Aggie on her feet and Leanna rushed forward to support her.

"Hand her over, Miss Cahill…if you please." Van Slyck was not making a request.

Standing in the glow of the back porch lamp stood a man who nodded his head with a pair of double chins flapping. This must be the owner of Hell's Corner Saloon, the man who wanted to hurt Cabe.

He would deal with these men later. Right now, getting Aggie out of here was urgent.

Cleve intercepted Van Slyck's move toward Leanna and Aggie. He glowered and bunched his fists.

The coward took a hasty step backward.

"You may have a contract," Cleve stated. "What Miss Cahill and I have is a moral obligation."

"Enforce that." Van Slyck snickered.

Cleve grabbed his lapels and jerked him off balance. His eyes grew wide. Moonlight glinted off a gold fleck in one of his eyes.

Cleve punched the smirk off his face with a well-placed blow to the gut. He grabbed Van Slyck by his expensive lapels again.

"Cleve, let's go." Leanna tugged on his sleeve.

"Never, ever let Miss Cahill's son's name come out of your mouth again…and tell the same to the fellow who just skedaddled back inside."

Cleve shoved, sending the natty Mr. Preston Van Slyck butt-first onto a mud puddle. That, he figured, was where the swine belonged.

Chapter Eight

A rifle shot cracked over the meadow behind the house, followed by another and then three more. Five cans tumbled from a boulder in the distance.

Sweat dampened Leanna's collar but she didn't unbutton it. If she could manage an accurate aim with her clothes feeling like a furnace against her skin, she could easily bring down anyone threatening Boodle, be it in the pits of Hades or Cahill Crossing.

At eight in the morning, the sun was scorching and the air so humid that breathing felt like sucking hot mist instead of air.

She inhaled a lungful of late-August misery, then fired another shot.

The remaining can spun through the air. It landed in the grass beside the others. The very last thing she wanted to do was walk all the way to the boulder and set them straight again, but she did it, four more times.

Years ago, following Chance about the countryside, watching him shoot and copying him, had been fun. Never in her life had she expected to wound more than a tin of beans.

Today, her aim was as true as it had been back then. Chance would be pleased to know that his instructions had held over time. But shooting a can was a different thing from shooting a man. If the moment came, would she be able to do it?

She stroked the polished butt of the Winchester, feeling the smooth wood slide over her palm.

Without a doubt, if her son were in danger. She wouldn't waste a heartbeat on regret. Her aim would be deadly.

Last night she had come home, knelt beside her bed and prayed that the owner of Hell's Corner Saloon hadn't meant what he'd said about harming Boodle. She'd prayed that Preston had actually been horrified that the man would consider it.

But he had laughed, and callously, so she hadn't slept a wink the whole livelong night. With every fading star she'd mentally cleaned her dusty rifle, sighted an imaginary evil poking its head up here or peeping around a corner there, and fired at it…over and over.

"I reckon you could shoot down that butterfly dipping over the meadow if you tried."

"Cleve!" Leanna spun about. "I didn't hear you coming."

He walked toward her across wilted grass. Funny, just the fact that he was nearby made everything feel not quite so alarming. The shadows and worrisome thoughts that had plagued her during the night scattered at his smile.

"It's been a while since I held a weapon like that one," he said. "Mind if I have a go?"

She handed him the rifle. He held it for a moment, turning it this way and that, as though becoming reacquainted with an old ally.

"Years ago, back on the homestead, I kept a weapon like this one close at hand…couldn't have been more than twelve." He aimed, shot a can off the rock, then grinned at her. "I suppose there are some things you don't forget."

"Like love of the land," she said, reading the pensive look on his face.

He nodded. "Like the soil prepared for planting… the way it feels when you rub it between your fingers."

"And the dust cloud that lifts from the ground when a herd of horses is running free," she added.

Cleve was silent for a moment, gazing at her and probably lost in memories, the same as she was.

"I challenge you to a contest," she said to break the spell of the past. "Let's see who misses a tin can first."

"I'll take that challenge." He handed her the rifle. "If you win, I give you a kiss."

"If you win, I give you—" she began.

"Two," he countered.

"All right…two kisses if you win." She aimed the gun and shot her can off the boulder.

"The first one, sweet." His grin flickered at her in a not-so-sweet way. "And the second…let's just say that your brothers won't approve."

He fired and knocked his can from its perch.

He was nearly her match with the weapon, but his shots tended toward the top or bottom of the can while hers went straight through the middle.

If she won this competition there would be only the one sweet kiss. She was far past telling herself that it was enough.

On her next turn she sharpened her aim…a quarter inch past the edge of the can. The bullet buried into the hillside behind the boulder with a puff of dust.

"Looks like you lose," Cleve said, the crease in his cheek lifted.

"Then I'll be forced to pay my debt." She stepped close to him and set the rifle down in the grass.

"I won't go easy on you." He cupped her face.

She sighed against his lips.

If there was a first, sweet kiss, she failed to notice it. The second kiss made the world fall away. His mouth claimed her, deep and hard. It twirled her belly. It made parts of her twist and throb that had never twisted and throbbed before.

She moaned when she feared he might pull away. His mouth stole her breath, but it kidnapped her heart.

The heart, that for so long had beat lonely and vulnerable, felt safe for the first time since her parents' deaths.

Cleve made her feel that way. He might not feel for her the way a husband ought to, but he would provide sanctuary for her and her son.

He'd promised and she believed him.

"Cleve," she whispered against his cheek. "Ask me to marry you."

He took her face between his big hands, gazing down at her. His eyes shimmered with the morning heat. Even though he didn't love her, his expression said that she had just handed him the world.

"Will you marry me, Leanna? Be my wife and you'll never be sorry. You won't need to shoot cans off a rock. I'll be here to watch over you and Cabe…I promise to give you that. I know I can't offer you everything you want…not now, but I will cherish you, and I'll be faithful. I'll be the best man I can be."

"I'll marry you." Cleve looked as pleased as a man who had just won a woman he really did love. She could nearly pretend…

"You won't be sorry. We'll build a good life, you, me and little Cabe."

"Let's buy a ranch, a pretty piece of ground to be

our own?" He would want that as much as she did, she was certain.

"I'll give you anything that's in my power to give, Leanna."

"I won't expect you to— I'll understand that you can't—" She sighed. A woman couldn't very well ask for future love. It had to come on its own or not at all. "I'll ask you for honesty and for respect. I reckon a marriage can begin with that, then who's to guess where it might go from there?"

His smile faded. He looked suddenly somber.

"I'll be the best husband I can be. We share a dream, and this…" He kissed her until she couldn't breathe. "It's a bond as strong as any other."

"I'm coming to believe that, but still, give me the truth and I'll give it to you. It shows, at least, that we respect each other."

That would mean she would have to tell him everything. In exchange for his protection, in the hopes that passion would sow the seeds of love, she would trust him with her future and her secrets.

He answered by drawing her close and burying his face in her neck. She replied by turning her head and finding his mouth.

She did love Cleve. With every moment, she felt that certainty settle more deeply in her heart. One day, he might love her with his heart as well as his hands. But for this very instant his hands gave her what she needed.

"This might be enough," she admitted.

Then he took her down into the dry scratchy grass where they celebrated in a tangle of sweat and heavy breathing.

A week later, heat still smothered the earth. It was all anyone could talk about. Crops wilted without rain. Birds perched in trees with their small beaks hanging open. Dogs lay in the shade panting while, from one end of town to the other, folks grumbled.

Cleve paced behind Leanna's house, the house he would be moving into tonight. His jacket hung on a tree limb so that it wouldn't be soaked with sweat the way his shirt was. With the ceremony only moments away, he wanted to look presentable for his bride. He couldn't give her much, but he could give her a decent appearance.

He longed to take a dip in the stream, but walking beside it would have to do.

A movement from Leanna's bedroom window caught his attention. Cassie carried something frothy and cream-colored across his line of sight. Leanna's wedding veil.

Exclamations of feminine delight floated down to him.

In the seven days since Leanna had accepted his proposal, he had asked himself the same question a hundred times.

The argument always went: Was he doing the right thing? He didn't know, but he was doing the best thing. Were his motives for giving his bride less than she dreamed of good enough? It was her own son, more or less, that he meant to protect by reciting the vows. That counted in his favor.

The last thing he had intended when he came to Cahill Crossing was to take a wife. He'd only wanted to take a child.

Wasn't it better this way? He cared for Leanna too deeply to take the boy away, and little Cabe had never known another mother. Any other course of action would cause hearts to be broken beyond repair.

Cleve crouched down at the stream bank to let the water trickle around his fingers.

His internal argument always ended the same way. He was doing the only thing he could for the good of everyone, particularly himself. Cabe Cahill was his flesh and blood and he meant to raise him, no matter what.

As reasonable as his arguments were, one thing continued to plague him. In a few moments Leanna Cahill would become Leanna Holden, his flesh and blood as much as his nephew was.

Truth was the one thing his bride had asked of him. He should have given her that from the first moment she asked it, but he had been a coward. Had he told her then who he was and why he'd come to Cahill Crossing, the odds were heavy that she would not have married him.

The time might well come when she made that discovery.

He stood to lose everything if she did.

He wouldn't think about that now because when

he'd told Leanna that he might be able to love her, it hadn't been idle words to get her to say yes. Quite honestly, he was halfway there now. His admiration of her had settled deep in his heart.

From this day forward, his life would never be the same. Whether he loved his wife or not, the world would be a cold place without her.

"Mr. Holden, may I have a word?"

"Dorothy," he said, standing and shaking the water from his fingertips. "That wedding feast you've been working on smells fit for President Chester Arthur."

"Don't try and flatter me out of what I've come to say."

"That wasn't flattery. Just the plain truth."

"Be that as it may, Cleve Holden, I've a thing or two to say."

"Words of advice for a nervous groom?"

"Words of warning, more like." Dorothy wiped the perspiration from her brow with the back of her hand. "Miss Leanna doesn't have her mama here to speak for her so I'm doing it."

"I'm glad you are."

"Well, we'll see about that. I hear her speaking to her mama at night so I know what's in her heart. She wants to be loved, more than most anything. Poor thing can't see how that will ever happen, though. She talks to her mama about you. She's marrying you but she wouldn't be if it weren't for her child—that's not what she says, just what I think. A woman, especially that one, ought to have what she wants."

"I'll make her as happy as I know how." He promised this to himself as well as to Dorothy.

"I told her she ought to marry you, true love or not. I even said that her mama would want that. Don't make me sorry." Dorothy's mouth set in a firm line, her arms crossed over the bodice of her respectable gray gown, made fancy for the ceremony by a wilted flower pinned to the collar.

"I intend to make Leanna the envy of Cahill Crossing."

"I hope that's enough."

"It had better be." Bowie's voice came from behind them. His boots crunched the dry grass. "Wedding's ready to begin."

"I'll leave you to your men talk, then." Dorothy turned and hurried for the house.

Cleve plucked his jacket from the tree branch and put it on. Silently, he walked beside Bowie toward the back door.

"Here's what I have to say," Bowie declared before they mounted the back steps. "I may be giving my sister away to you, but treat her wrong and I'll damned well take her back."

"You'd have to fight me for her."

Bowie grinned and slapped him on the back.

Leanna stood at the top of the parlor stairs with Bowie, watching the scene below through a veil of ivory gauze.

The sun had set. Lamps cast a romantic glow over

the parlor. Curtains fluttered inward on a breeze, damp with the promise of rain.

Cassie plunked out the wedding march on the slightly off-key piano that had come with the house.

In front of the hearth, Cleve stood beside the preacher. Only his smile, warm with promise, kept her from dashing back to her bedroom.

Maybe she ought to have revealed that she was a virgin before she recited her vows. She'd tried, a dozen times, but the words had remained stuck in her mouth, and her such a preacher for the truth.

Standing now at the top of the stairs, she wasn't certain if she was making the best decision of her life, or the worst. Marrying Cleve with this secret between them might doom the young marriage from the start.

Whether or not she descended the stairs on Bowie's arm came down to one decision.

How much did she trust Cleve?

Enough to let him discover the truth about her son? To put their fate in his hands?

The best thing might be to call the wedding off this very moment while there was still time. He didn't love her so he wouldn't be crushed. Maybe disappointed for a while, but he'd get over it. He'd find himself a decent woman.

He winked up at her. The crease in his cheek lifted with her smile.

And there it was... This truth hit her smack in the heart. She didn't want him with a decent woman.

Glancing up at Bowie, she nodded. He escorted her down the stairs.

The parlor was speckled with people who loved her. And one who admired her…greatly.

They stood in a half circle around Cleve and the preacher. Massie leaned shoulder to shoulder with Sam Webber. Lucinda and Dorothy dabbed at their eyes. Cabe and Melvin shuffled from foot to foot, sweating in their Sunday best and their attention focused on the wedding cake in the corner.

She was relieved to see Merritt Dixon with the group. They had not been friends in the past. Merritt had been a grieving widow while Leanna had been busy in her shallow world of parties and pretty gowns. How, she wondered, would Bowie's future wife feel about being her sister?

This concern flashed through her mind quickly. Her attention was all for her groom, grinning and waiting for her beside the preacher.

The holy vows took only a few moments to recite, but looking into Cleve's eyes, she meant each and every one of them…for a lifetime.

She would love Cleve with all her heart, even if he never loved her back.

Standing here before God and all these witnesses, she silently prayed that her groom had been right. That love could grow.

She was pretty sure she hadn't loved him last week, but right now, kissing him the second the preacher gave consent, she did. With blessings from above, and maybe a little help from Mama, her brand-new husband might come to feel the same way.

Dorothy rushed forward as soon as Cleve gave her a breath. With one hand still twined in her husband's, she hugged her friend.

"Your mama would want this," Dorothy whispered in her ear.

"I think so, too," she whispered back, and kissed Dorothy's cheek.

Next, Massie and Sam offered their good wishes. Lucinda and Cassie took turns embracing her while they sniffled and smiled.

Cabe and Melvin inched closer to the cake.

Last of all Bowie came forward with his intended.

Clearly, Merritt was no longer grieving. She was radiant with her hand tucked into the crook of Bowie's arm, as if that's the place she had belonged all her life.

Could she ever recall seeing that happiness on Bowie's face before? She could not.

"Annie, you remember Merritt?" Bowie said.

Merritt's eyes flashed a green twinkle and she opened her arms wide.

Leanna stepped into her hug. Already, she loved the woman who had put the joy in her brother's heart. Maybe she ought to have sought Merritt out as soon as she'd discovered her engagement to Bowie, but there was always the chance she might have shamed her by doing so.

If the strength of Merritt's embrace was anything

to go by, she didn't give a whit what decent folks might think.

Chance wasn't here, neither were Quin and Addie K., and she was sorry for that. Time and distance could not be helped, though.

And Ellie's absence? She was sorry for that, too. It stung even though she knew what consequences Ellie would have faced had she defied her mother.

In her way, Ellie was as dominated by her mother as the red-light ladies were by Preston and the Fitzgerald boys. Sadly, she had more power to help the doves than she did her own friend.

With the good wishes finished, Cleve whispered in her ear, his breath moist and warm against her upswept hair. "What do you say we eat Dorothy's meal, quick-like, give the boys their cake and then go upstairs, Mrs. Holden?"

"Dorothy's prepared a feast, so we'll have to linger awhile, but I'll admit—" she turned to face him, speaking low "—it's not food I'm hungry for."

Cleve laughed. The suggestive rumble fluttered her heart, but lower it did things that made her want to skip the meal and run up the stairs two at a time.

The house was as quiet as Leanna's held breath.

After the feasting and the many toasts to a long marriage and a dozen baby Holdens, the company, Cabe and Melvin among them, had gone to spend the night at the saloon, which was closed because it was Sunday.

Leanna sat on her bed. Cleve stood in front of her, his masculinity a contrast to the flowered frilliness of her bedroom. He gazed down at her with a look that, while not precisely love, held a good deal of simmering, seductive affection.

He unbuttoned his coat and set it on the bed behind her.

"I'm going to kiss you, Mrs. Holden." He removed his tie, then his shirt and laid them on top of the jacket. "Everywhere."

He began with her fingertips. Kneeling in front of her, he nibbled them one by one.

Now would be time to warn him that she was untouched.

Then again, it might be better to wait until after she discovered what the next place to be kissed would be.

Oh, the cleft of her elbow—how lovely.

The next instant wasn't the moment to admit her secret because his lips nuzzled the curve between her neck and her shoulder, and really, she'd like to feel that a moment longer before she spoke up.

His teeth nipped her earlobe at the same time he reached behind her to flick open the pearl buttons on the back of her wedding gown.

Air, heavy with heat and humidity, clung to her arms when he drew the gown away from her body. Fabric shifted and whispered, fluttering forward onto her lap. She lifted up to allow him to slide the garment to the floor. His fingers caressed a sultry path from hips, to calves, to ankles.

She nearly opened her mouth to reveal her secret but there was a chance that he would hate her desperately after she did. Her groom was entitled to the experienced, provocative woman he thought he'd married, not a quivering virgin, even if the virgin was not quivering with fear but instead with anticipation of what was coming next.

He pulled hairpins from the stylish mound of loops and whorls piled on top of her head.

"I've wondered what this would feel like." He drew the loose strands through his fingers, gathered the tresses to one side and smoothed them over her breast. Her nipple puckered against peekaboo lace and the hot palm of his hand.

It was nearly too late to make her confession now. She might as well wait until…

"Oh…mmm." The only thing her sigh confessed was that when his big hands circled her breasts, squeezed and caressed them though a veil of lace, she felt like a drowsy bee circling a honey pot.

This was the moment in time to reveal the truth. In another second he would taste the honey in her pot. He would discover the truth of her unsullied condition on his own and he might despise her.

To her dismay, her tongue and everything else had become too languid to move. He tugged on her camisole, exposing her breasts to the stuffy air and to his perusal.

"Cleve, I—" she managed.

"So do I, love, so do I."

Poor Cleve, he didn't; he only thought he did. She yanked the sheer fabric up. It didn't do much to hide her chest from his increasingly intimate stare.

"But, Cleve, it's raining."

Even though she would have sworn it to be impossible, she stood, hurried across the room and down the stairs.

A good drenching ought to shake the words out of her, or at least give her more time to consider them.

No matter what words she used, Cleve might leave her. When a man married a mother, the last thing he expected on his wedding night was a lying virgin.

Chapter Nine

Cleve dashed outside. Rain sheeted off the back porch roof. It pounded the ground. The welcome scent of wet earth made the temperature seem to dip.

Halfway across the yard, Leanna stood with her arms outstretched and her face tipped toward the sky. Just like the trees and the grass, she soaked up water. So did her camisole and her bloomers.

Cleve stepped out into the rain. Water ran down his bare chest and for the first time in days he was able to take a gulp of cool air.

He was a goat, a worm…a hypocrite of the worst kind. While Leanna was moments from revealing the secret of her virginity, he had determined that he might never admit his secret to her. If he did, it might damn him in her eyes.

He didn't want to be damned in her eyes. He wanted to look into them and see… Hell, he didn't know quite what it was he wanted to see, but it wasn't disfavor.

He watched his bride dance about the yard, probably not realizing that her underclothes had become translucent. It was a lucky thing that the nearest neighbor was a fair distance away and that visibility was impaired by the deluge.

Standing several feet away from Leanna doing her happy rain dance, he crossed his arms and smiled. The storm did only good things to his visibility.

He did know, after all, what he wanted to see in his bride's eyes—lust, burning blue-hot.

Her appreciation of the rain was infectious. He lifted his face. Cool, watery fingers washed over his eyes and nose; it soaked his hair.

New life had begun today. His, Leanna's and Cabe's—the promise of it was as fresh as the downpour.

Leanna would never be sorry she had married him; he'd make damn sure of that.

It wouldn't hurt a soul to keep his and Cabe's former relationship buried. Beginning today, he was no longer his uncle, but his father.

He lowered his head and opened his eyes. His bride stood motionless, staring at him with a big, doelike gaze.

Curly hair, raven-black with water sluicing over it, looped down her back. Sheer lace clung to her breasts; it kissed her where he longed to. Soggy embroidered roses circled her nipples with an invitation for him to pluck the pebbled bouquet.

"You are lovely, Leanna." The tightness in his throat choked his words.

The bloomers' gauzy shadow curved her backside; it stroked the slope of belly and hip.

She resembled a porcelain doll, luminous, with water glistening on every luscious swell and dip. And there, at the junction of her thighs was a curling, dripping nest of ebony hair that made his blood slide from his heart downward.

Wet grass tickled in between his bare toes when he closed the distance between them. He slid his hand around the back of her neck. "Come back upstairs."

He pressed her to him, lifting her so that they were heartbeat to heartbeat.

He kissed her and tasted cool water on her mouth.

She melted against him, like a flame dancing in the storm and defying it.

Without warning, she shoved against his chest, slid down and took a long step backward. "There's something I have to tell you."

He grabbed her hand and pulled her back. "Not now."

"But, Cleve, it's important." She tried to wriggle out of his grip so he kissed her again.

For an instant she allowed it, but in the end, she turned her head. "I've kept a secret from you…. I didn't give birth to Cabe."

Here was the conversation he'd sought since he

first set foot in Cahill Crossing, but at this instant, it was the last thing he wanted to hear.

"I know I should have told you sooner. I wanted to, but I had to know I could trust you and..." Moisture misted her eyes. "The fact is I do and now I'm sorry I didn't—"

"That's not important right now," he heard his voice whisper, quite shocked that it was true. "Tonight, not a damn thing exists but you and me and that bed upstairs."

"But, Cleve! I'm a virgin."

He swept her up in his arms, feeling the slick slide of soaked lace against his skin.

"Not for long."

"But, Cleve," Leanna whispered when her husband lay her down on her...their...bed and covered her with himself. "Don't you care that I lied to you?"

He paused with his fingers tangled in the waistband of her bloomers.

"What you did is keep a secret." He rolled off her to lie beside her, his belly to her hip. He pulled the drawstring from her drawers, leaving the lace slack and gaping. He stroked her belly. "We all have them."

"But don't you want to—" his fingers circled downward; one of them dipped into her feminine spot, still circling "—to... I can't think when you do that."

"Good, you aren't supposed to." With his free hand he cupped her breast, then rolled her nipple between his fingers. "We'll think later. Right now, it's about you and me and carnal knowledge."

"I believe that I could become fond of carnal knowledge." She didn't think about doing it, but she moved her hips, seeking deeper pleasure.

Cleve made a sound deep in his chest, something like a lion's purr and her name.

She wasn't finished speaking. She wanted to assure him that this closeness would be enough to base a marriage on, for now at least, but her thoughts fled. Existence narrowed to Cleve Holden, the scent of him, the sound of his breath in her ear and the seduction of his circling finger urging her to lay her heart at his feet.

The only word she knew in that moment was *Cleve*. Moaned and not spoken.

Lightning flashed outside, spearing the room with shattered light. Lightning flashed inside her, shattering her with pleasure, then leaving her pulsing in its ebb.

Wind hit the side of the house and blew rain through the open window into the room. It pattered on the rug where Cleve stood, stepping out of his trousers. He slipped off his drawers.

Thunder tumbled across the roof. Water drops pebbled over her groom's skin. They hung like tiny diamonds on his chest and the muscled lines of his belly. Her husband was a wonderful sight, lean and hard everywhere...absolutely everywhere.

Crawling over her on the bed, his knees brushed

the inside of her thighs, nudging them. One part of him that was hard was also heavy. It grazed her mound, stiff and fever-hot. She gasped at what that sensation did to her, what it made her want to do.

Virgin or not, she knew to splay her thighs for him, her husband.

When he filled her, stretched her, passion sweltered white-hot; it intoxicated. He moved within her and she answered him. When he shattered, she shattered.

She came to herself with his weight sprawled across her and her name on his lips, his breath stirring her hair.

As of this moment, she was Leanna Holden in name and deed. Even more, she was Leanna Holden in her heart.

She loved Cleve, and for now, the joining of their bodies would be enough.

It would not be enough forever, but for now, she would be content to be taught the art of carnal knowledge.

Leanna slept with her head on his chest, her bare shoulder half-covered by her hair. He stroked the dark strands between his fingers, smoothing the curls, then letting them spring back into place.

He tugged her in close with both arms to better feel the rise and fall of her breathing.

Even now, after the night they had spent, he could scarcely believe she was his.

They had made love all through the wee hours. Sometimes he took her as wildly as the storm still pounding the house. Other times he took her sweetly and tenderly, but in the end, she was the one to have taken him. Each and every time she sighed or gasped his name she staked her claim deeper in his heart.

If the choice were his, he would hold this moment, just the two of them warm and sated while the storm blustered against the closed window. Life wasn't in the habit of waiting, though. Dawn would bring things that needed facing.

Many of them wonderful. His nephew was now his to raise, his wife his to…to care for deeply.

One thing was not wonderful. He kept a secret that he regretted keeping. It was as risky as four of a kind in a cheater's hand with the fifth already on the table.

He'd told Leanna that love could grow. But so fast? He didn't think so. What he felt in this moment had to be the result of admiration and lust, tinder to flint, spreading like wildfire.

If the day came that he fell in love with his wife, he would be vulnerable in a way that he had never been before. He'd seen the results of love gone wrong. Hadn't that ultimately killed his little sister?

If Leanna ever discovered that he was Cabe's uncle she wouldn't forgive him and he wouldn't blame her. When a woman married a protector, she didn't want a goat and a worm. When she inevitably left him, he might recover from caring deeply, but not from loving her with a full heart.

The wedding night had been perfect. He'd chase the dawn away with his bare fists if he could, but it was on its way along with the return of the people who lived in this house.

The very last thing he wanted right now was to know how his sister had died, but some things had to be faced.

"Leanna," he whispered in her ear. Her lips tickled his shoulder when she smiled. "Wake up, love."

She stretched both arms over her head and blinked her eyes. One perfectly mounded, well-tended breast peeped out from under the blanket.

"Um." She sighed. "Please don't say it's morning already."

"Not quite." He sat up and leaned back against the headboard. Hell, he didn't want to do this. "I'd like to hear the story of how you became an untouched mother."

Leanna sighed. She sat up and propped a pillow between her back and the headboard. She handed one to him, then drew the blanket to her chin.

"If you aren't Cabe's mama, who is?" he asked with all the innocence he could fabricate.

Here was the beginning of deceptions. He would listen to the story of Arden's tragic end, nodding and holding back emotion as though his sister had been a stranger.

"Don't hate me, Cleve." She glanced up sideways at him and made him feel worse than a low-down worm.

"I suppose you had good reasons for taking the boy."

"His mother gave him to me."

He'd figured as much, but he needed to hear the story and all the while put on the face of a common, concerned stranger.

"Since I'm Cabe's papa now, I ought to know what happened."

"I'm glad you are his papa." She squeezed his hand under the covers.

He was glad to be raising the boy, more than he could let on.

"I met Arden Honeybee—that's his mama's name—in Deadwood."

He had so many questions that he could not ask. Did she ever speak of her brother? That one haunted him.

"Honeybee went in place of her last name. So many of the women were too ashamed to reveal their family name—Arden was one of those."

"Poor thing," he said casually. "I wonder if she had a family."

"I asked her. She said she didn't, but she'd have said that, regardless."

Apparently, his bride didn't notice how pain had turned him rigid beside her. She went on with the story without hesitation.

"I don't want you to think badly of Arden, Cleve.

She was a good and decent woman before society turned against her."

"If she'd had family, they might have helped her."

"Most wouldn't. Arden came to Deadwood hoping to find honest work, but that's not an easy thing for a woman, even a healthy one. Poor Arden was far from healthy."

"That's sad." He would have helped her; he wanted to shout it but couldn't.

"Tragic is what…and so very sad. There was a time when Arden had been happy and in love, looking forward to getting married, even."

"Did she say what happened?"

Leanna nodded. "The fellow was a beast. He used her and left her."

"You said one time that he didn't know that he had fathered a child."

"It doesn't make him less of a beast."

"It makes him more of one. He should have been certain before he went on his way. You ought to tell me who he is."

"Not more than I ought to keep my promise to my dying friend."

Her words brought a picture to his mind that was too hard to take sitting down. He got up and walked naked to the window, staring at the rain-streaked windowpane without seeing it.

"Maybe we shouldn't open the saloon today," he mumbled, just to have something to say. "The storm keeps getting worse."

"Maybe… Come back to bed, Cleve, you look chilled."

He was, but not the way she thought. She lifted her arms and he returned to the bed.

"Then what happened?" He settled beside her.

"Arden serviced the men at the saloon where I dealt cards. It wasn't the most awful place she could have worked, but she grew sicker as time went on. Not many men take to a sick whore, especially one whose belly is swollen."

Cleve nodded because his voice failed him.

"I took her home with me to Mrs. Jameston's boardinghouse. I tried to get her to eat and take care of herself, but she only got weaker. We were close. I loved Arden like I would have loved a sister. She didn't think she would survive the birth. I told her she would, even though we both knew she wouldn't. She begged me to love her baby and raise it as my own…. Cleve…I tried so hard to get her to live."

Leanna wiped her cheek, dashing away tears. His throat cramped with a sob but he couldn't do a blessed thing about it.

"In the end she didn't survive long enough even to hold her child. She died the very instant he came. Her last cry was his first. I can't tell you how I felt in that moment. A life gone and a life begun…such loss and joy all at the same time."

Leanna turned her face into his shoulder and wept. After a moment she looked at him with red-rimmed eyes.

"I might have been the one giving birth that night for all the love and pain. And I do love Arden's boy that much."

Cleve tipped his head, resting his cheek on Leanna's hair. "Thank you for telling me."

"You would have discovered I wasn't anyone's mother on your own."

She snuggled into him and, amazingly, the ache in his soul eased. It hurt to know the truth, but the shadows that had plagued him for years began to lift.

"I knew you weren't Cabe's mother."

"What?" She pushed away from him with small, warm hands. "How could you?"

"Fallen women don't blush. You, my love, have the prettiest pink one, right there, just across the bridge of your nose."

He traced the rosy-tinged flesh with his finger, down her neck and over the swell of her chest.

"It'll be daylight soon." She sighed.

He tugged her down to the mattress.

"Not for a while, yet."

Chapter Ten

Leanna sat on a chair in Doc Lewis's waiting room gazing through the open window at the sunny afternoon. Warm air drifted inside carrying the scent of jasmine from a vine trained around the window frame. The voices of children playing nearby filtered in with it.

The examination room door opened. Doc Lewis stepped out. He glanced behind him, then closed the door with a quiet click.

"I'm glad you brought Aggie in, Mrs. Holden," he said.

"I'm worried, Doctor." Doc Lewis pulled a chair from against the far wall and sat down across from her. "It's been close to two weeks and she seems the same as the day Cleve and I...well, what we did is we—"

"Rescued her?" Doc supplied, arching his brows over friendly brown eyes.

"Not everyone calls it that."

"Miss Aggie does." The doctor rested his elbows on his knees and linked his fingers together. "You shouldn't pay any mind to what a few folks have to say."

Leanna sighed. She used to care. Somehow, the opinions of busybodies didn't matter so much anymore. That's what she needed to teach her girls.

Especially Aggie. Her rescue had not been cheered by most of the residents of Cahill Crossing. Preston had used his vicious tongue to drop a word here and a rumor there, saying that Aggie was vile and ruined beyond redemption.

How odd that no one thought badly of Preston for being in a position to be familiar with Aggie's ruin. No doubt his dashing looks and his engaging smile forgave him. The fact that he was the banker's son gave him an aura of respectability no matter what.

"Thank you for seeing Aggie, Doctor." Leanna opened her bag to pay him but Doc Lewis stayed her hand.

"Aggie can pay me when she is able."

"Hopefully, one day she will be able to. Right now, I hardly know what to do for her. She barely eats. She jumps at every noise and only speaks when she is asked a question."

"She's been wounded inside. Being treated like she has, and for a good many years, it's going to take time."

A baseball sailed through the open window and

Doc Lewis caught it easily, then tossed it back as though he had done it dozens of times before.

"Thanks, Doc," called a young boy's voice.

"Keep her mind stimulated. Try not to let her close up on herself. Her body is healing fine but the brain and the heart work in ways that we simple doctors don't understand."

Leanna stood; so did Doc Lewis.

"Don't hesitate to bring her back if you need to."

"I'll do that, and thank you again."

"Married life must agree with you, Mrs. Holden. You look the picture of health."

He was right, marriage did agree with her. August had turned into September and still, two weeks later, the days were wonderful and the nights were too sultry even to think about in front of good Doc Lewis.

"If you need my services on your own behalf, I hope you won't be too shy."

Leanna nodded, even though she was no doubt turning six shades of crimson.

"Good. It's important to be seen once a month during your time. Most mothers only call me when the child is coming, but regular care is vital. A lot of heartache could be prevented...well, there I go preaching again, but it is important."

"If that time comes, you'll see me," Leanna vowed, and meant it. Would Arden be alive today had she been in the care of Doc Lewis?

Doc Lewis opened the examination room door

and escorted Aggie out. She avoided his touch and stared down at the floor.

Leanna took her arm and led her across the room.

"If you need anything, Miss Holt, I'll be here, day or night." The doctor opened the front door. "Good afternoon, ladies."

"Thank you, Dr. Lewis," Aggie murmured without lifting her gaze from the polished floorboards.

Outside, the afternoon was sunny, full of birdsong, laughing children and hope.

"Aggie, we're going by the bank on the way home."

Aggie stiffened beside her. "Folks will stare. I can't do it."

"They might stare, they might do worse." Leanna tipped Aggie's chin so that sunlight shone on her pale frightened face. "Shoulders square, my friend, I've got you. Besides, I'm the one who gave my son a gambler for a father. Those stares will likely be at me."

"But, Miss Cahill, Preston might be there."

"That is precisely why we are going. Preston preys on weak women. You and I are going to show him that we are not weak."

"I am. All I want to do is run home and lock my bedroom door."

Leanna squeezed Aggie's arm, relieved to hear her voice an opinion at last. For nearly three weeks she had done nothing more than nod and mumble.

"So do I, but locking ourselves away is no way to live."

The walk from Doc Lewis's office to the bank was short, just around the south side of Town Square and past the town hall. Along the way she spoke to Aggie about calico dresses, hair ribbons and hatpins.

A few rude stares greeted them and Leanna had to remind Aggie to look up, not at her shuffling feet.

Entering the bank was a relief, even though Preston sat behind his desk looking like the answer to every mama's prayer.

"Mrs. Holden." Willem Van Slyck stood up from his desk. He strode forward to greet her, speaking through the bars that separated the back room of the bank from the lobby. "It's a pleasure. How may I help you?"

"Let me, Father. I'd be delighted to assist the ladies." No one could have missed the sneer in Preston's voice.

"Sit down, Preston," Willem ordered, slashing a frown at his son. "How can I help you, Leanna?"

He could help her by revealing what he knew about Mama's and Papa's deaths. She looked Willem hard in his gold-flecked eye; she glanced at Preston, but if they kept secrets it didn't show. Willem appeared to be the soul of civility and Preston hid his malice behind a handsome grin.

The office, though, was full of files. If she could get to them, paper and ink wouldn't lie. She had no idea what she ought to search for, but that wouldn't keep her from looking.

"Miss Holt would like to open an account." Leanna drew twenty dollars from her reticule and placed it on the counter.

This was Aggie's first step away from her old life. It had been Leanna's intention to have Preston witness that step. No matter what, he would not have the poor girl back. He would not have any woman who came to Hearts for Harlots for help.

If Leanna wasn't mistaken, Preston had just bitten his tongue. Even the congenial crinkle of his eyes couldn't hide his attempt to smother his anger.

She smiled sweetly at him and he scowled back.

A challenge issued and accepted.

Cleve knelt before a bush in front of the house with Cabe squatting beside him. He pointed at a blinking spot on a leaf.

"Look there, son, that's a firefly. Tomorrow night I'll show you how to catch them and put them in a jar."

"Fly," Cabe repeated. He reached a chubby fist toward the bug but it flitted away out of reach. He pointed at Cleve's nose. "Papa."

"That's right, little man. I'm your papa and no one else."

The rustle of a silk skirt and the squeak of the screen door drew his attention up to the porch.

"Thank you for that, Cleve." Leanna leaned over

the railing. "Mama and Papa have to go to work now, Boodle. We'll see you in the morning."

Leanna came down the stairs, picked up Cabe, then carried him to Dorothy, who waited on the top step.

Cleve stood and straightened his jacket. He took Leanna's hand and tucked it into the crook of his arm while they walked past the school.

"I love September," his wife said, gazing up at the dark sky all speckled with stars. "Fall's on the way and a body can nearly smell it. Maybe Chance will come home soon."

"Leanna, don't thank me for being a daddy to Cabe. He's a fine boy. I thank you for trusting me with him."

"It wasn't easy for me, marrying for the reasons we did, but now that it's done, I'm glad. I don't know who I would want to raise him more than you."

At the edge of the schoolyard Cleve stopped and kissed her.

"I didn't marry you just for Cabe's sake." He tucked her hand back into the bend of his arm and walked on with his lips bent down to her ear. Not that anyone would hear him, but because of the feeling of intimacy that came with the whisper. "How late are we working tonight?"

"One o'clock, or until the customers are gone."

"Too long. Meet me in the back room closet at ten?"

"Nine forty-five."

He picked her up, hugged her tight, then twirled her around once with her feet and skirt flying.

"Cleve, there's something I want to do tonight and I'll need your help," she said when he set her down.

"Anything," he answered.

"I want to break into the bank."

"Anything but that." He tucked her hand once more into the crook of his arm and quickened his pace toward the gambling hall.

"But, Cleve," she panted, trying to match his long strides. He needed to get to the saloon quickly, before she hoodwinked him into some sort of scheme that would get them both thrown into jail. "I need to find out if those Van Slycks did something to Mama and Papa."

"What do you expect to find?" He slowed his pace. This was important to her even if breaking into the bank was the last thing he would allow her to do. "Even if they did have something to do with it, they wouldn't have left clues in the bank."

"They might not think they did, but I'm sure going to find that out for myself."

"No, you are not." With his mind spinning, he came upon the back door of the saloon with no sense of time passing. "If I have to tie you to a chair." A sudden erotic picture flashed in his mind, distracting him for an instant. Leanna, secured to the chair wearing nothing but a scowl. He shook his head to clear the image. "You are not breaking into the bank."

Leanna sighed and frowned. "I suppose I did vow

to obey you. Very well, then, I won't break into the bank."

"You can listen in on Van Slyck all evening if you want to. He's bound to let something slip."

"No doubt, since he hasn't come close to revealing a thing the whole livelong time I've been spying on him." Leanna smiled. She patted his cheek. "Tonight is surely the night he'll let something slip. Why bother with the bank?"

Her agreeable attitude sent a chill clear to his bones.

Waiting for Cleve to go upstairs and take his nightly break felt like waiting for water to boil; the longer she anticipated it, the less likely it seemed.

She strolled past a table that was a few feet from what had come to be known as Willem's chair. Van Slyck sat in it night after night, from exactly eight-thirty until precisely eleven-thirty.

More often than not Don Fitzgerald visited with him.

Like every other evening, the pair discussed the weather and a dozen other topics that had nothing to do with her parents.

What was Bowie thinking, asking her to listen in? The very last thing Van Slyck would talk about was how he had murdered the Cahills. That was even less likely than leaving an account of it at the bank.

Hearing nothing of interest beyond September

being especially cool this year, she crossed the room and sat down in a chair beside Aggie.

She had hoped that the sunflowers in the fireplace might cheer Aggie, or watching people come and go might ignite a spark of interest in her eye.

But no—the woman sat gazing at the rug as though her future might be revealed in the weave, and if it were, she didn't much care.

Leanna's attempted conversation with her amounted to a few nods and one-word answers to her questions. How she longed to march her over to Willem and Don and declare, *Look what your sons have done!*

She couldn't, of course. Chances are the men had no control over their offspring, anyway.

Leanna glanced up. Cleve had taken his break. She should have been paying attention! He would be upstairs for less than an hour. That barely gave her the time she needed to get to the bank, search it and rush back.

Casually, she walked into the back room. She rooted through the box of tools beside the door, then dashed down the steps. She wished she had taken the time to bring her wrap; the late-summer night had a nip to it.

She gathered her hem above her knees with one hand and the metal bar that she used for opening crates in the other.

Then she ran.

Even though, at this time of night in this part of

town, no one was about, she was glad she had chosen to wear a black dress to commit her crime. She ought to look like a mere shadow drifting through the night.

She formed a plan as she hurried across the Fort Ridge Road. She paused to catch her breath behind lawyer Slocum's office.

Drat Cleve for not agreeing to help her. The only way of breaking the lock on the back door of the bank was with the metal bar. Her husband would have the strength to make quick work of it, but she was in for a struggle.

She gripped the bar in both hands and crept forward with her unwieldy skirt shoved between her elbow and ribs.

Her plan was simple. Break the lock or break the window.

Shattering glass might make noise but would anyone hear it? Someone working late at the newspaper office, perhaps. This undertaking was not without risk. Still, she needed to find out what Van Slyck, be it father or son, knew.

She dearly hoped to discover Preston worthy of some crime that would put him behind bars. She longed to make him pay for what he had done to Arden, Aggie and who knew how many others? Locked in jail tight as a rusted screw, he'd never discover the secret she had been keeping from him.

Tap, tap, tap.

A noise pinged close by. She froze, listening.

Tap...tap...tap, the sound came again, and unless

she missed her bet it was coming from the rear of the bank, maybe even the back door.

She hadn't anticipated a bank robber, but if he broke the lock first she could simply wait until he had finished his business, then go in after him.

She let go of her skirt but held on tight to the bar. On tiptoe, she trotted the short distance between the back of the lawyer's office and a tall bush only yards away from the bank's back door.

Tap. Tap. Tap.

She parted the shrubbery and saw the thief kneeling in deep shadow beside the door, holding a hammer and a pick. This might take some time.

The lock wouldn't be as heavy as the one on the safe, but still, her bar would be more efficient than that constant tapping.

The thief paused in his work. He drew a watch from his vest and peered closely at it.

Perhaps he had another business to rob in a timely manner. Perhaps he... Leanna poked her head out of the shrub. She peered hard at the man.

"Cleve Holden!" she growled. She broke through the branches and stomped across the clearing, swatting dried leaves from her skirt and hair. "What are you doing here?"

He pivoted on his knee. "More to the point, what are *you* doing here?"

"Move over, Cleve." She nudged him aside. "You'll never get anything done with that little tool."

Leanna pried at the lock with her bar.

"Give me that." Cleve grabbed the bar and delivered the lock a good bashing.

Lantern light flared to life in the bank's rear window. Footsteps crossed the floor.

Cleve snagged her waist and rolled with her around the corner of the building half an instant before the back door banged open.

"Who's out there?" Preston's voice shot into the dark. "Show yourself!"

Praise everything that the moon was hidden behind clouds tonight. Cleve crouched in front of her, bar and pick at the ready.

"Is it my uncle?" a woman's voice came from inside, sounding fretful.

"Lilly Mae, I can hear your uncle snoring in his bed from a block away."

"Oh! A bank robber?"

"Where is the brain behind that pretty face?" Preston muttered, then louder said, "Don't worry yourself, sweet. Bank robbers come during bank hours so that someone is there to open the safe."

"If nobody's there, come back to bed," Lilly Mae's voice whined. "It's getting cold...and lonely."

"Better watch out, Father," Preston murmured, but being only a couple feet away his voice carried around the corner of the building as clear as a ringing bell. "Might be that someone's scratching for your secrets."

Cleve ushered Leanna into the closet of the saloon's back room and slammed the door. He pressed her against the wall between a broom and a mop. A pail hanging on a hook clattered when his elbow knocked it.

Darkness so complete that it prevented him from seeing his wife's expression wrapped them up. At least he could pretend that she was intimidated by his temper and half-sorry for disobeying him.

Her breathing came quick. Her cheeks, secured between his palms, flushed warm with excitement.

"Willem has secrets!" Her voice tickled his face. He wanted to make love to her, and badly, but first she had to understand that she could not put herself in danger the way she had.

"Everyone does. His secrets might not have any-thing to do with your parents." He slid his hands down her neck to grip her shoulders where her gown sagged off of them.

"If you believe that, why were you there?"

His wife's flesh felt like velvet beneath his thumbs. Almost, but not quite, against his will, he stroked her skin from collarbone to breastbone.

"Because I'm your husband and since I forbade you to break into the bank I had to do it myself."

"As sweet as that was, you can't forbid me."

He could damn well try. "What was that you promised in our marriage vows? As I recall, it was… to obey?"

"Really, Cleve." Heaven help him if she hadn't just chuckled under her breath. "No one means that. It's just something old and pretty to say. It's tradition."

He felt her hands reach down to touch him through his trousers. He dug deep for the force of will to make it through this lecture with his pants on.

"Here is my tradition—when I marry a woman, she is mine to protect and I can't do it if she goes off willy-nilly whenever she wants to."

"You've never been married before. You can't have a tradition already." There went button number one on his fly.

"Leanna, are you trying to drive me insane?"

"I'm only trying to find out what happened to Mama and Papa."

"And I will help you with that, I promise, but you have got to promise me that you won't put yourself in dangerous situations."

There went the rest of the buttons. He could have refastened them, but didn't.

"I promise I won't put myself in danger...intentionally."

"You'll be the death of me, love."

Since that was as much of a promise as he was going to get he gripped her silk skirt in his fists and gathered it up inch by inch. He nipped her shoulder. A shiver pebbled her flesh so he blew on it, whispering her name, to warm and smooth the chill.

"I think you care for me." Her head tipped back against the wall and he nibbled his way up her throat.

"You know I do."

"I think you love me."

He'd give his life for her...in a heartbeat. Just

this second, though, with her fingers stroking him, scrambling his brain, he couldn't ponder on what that might mean.

Chapter Eleven

Leanna lifted the lace doily on her dresser top and peered under it. The pink teacup sitting between her brush and her comb was empty. It should have contained the gold bracelet that Chance had given her for her sixteenth birthday.

The one that she had been wearing last night.

She searched the floor around the dresser, then under the bed. On hands and knees, she ran her fingers against the nap of the rug in the middle of the room.

"Cleve, wake up."

She glanced at the bed where Cleve's bare self lay with the embroidered coverlet across his hips and one finely muscled leg on top of it. Midmorning sunlight pierced the lace curtain and cast a rose-and-lattice pattern across his face.

He blinked one eye open, then patted the mattress.

"It can't be more than seven o'clock. Take off that corset, Mrs. Holden, and come back to bed."

"Don't tempt me. I'm taking the ladies to the general store this morning. Besides, it's nearly nine."

Leanna stood. She crossed to the armoire scanning the floor while she walked. She pulled out a fresh petticoat and wriggled it over her hips.

"Don't torture me." Cleve sat up, setting his feet on the floor and his elbows on his knees. He rubbed his sleepy-looking face between his palms.

Two hundred pounds of muscled male, speckled with shadow roses from the curtain, beckoned her.

"We worked late last night." He arched his brows and flipped back the coverlet. "The ladies are probably asleep."

"The boys won't be." Leanna shook her head. "We might have a problem."

She drew a simple but well-made plaid skirt over her head and buttoned it at her waist.

"The very last thing that you and I have is a problem." Cleve shot her a grin. He stood.

Well, he was right, of course, about that. They had made love into the wee hours of the morning, and still, here he was striding toward her, his torture evident.

She drew her arms through the sleeves of a demure white blouse and buttoned it to the chin.

"Sometime last night, I lost my bracelet."

"I suspect we'll find it in the broom closet." He

stood in front of her with his hands on her shoulders. He dipped his head and brushed the tip of his nose to hers. "Don't worry."

"I wouldn't, if it didn't have my initials on it."

Cleve reached behind her and yanked a shirt and pants out of the armoire. "I'll go back to the bank and have a look."

"Be careful, Cleve."

He kissed her while shoving his right arm through his shirtsleeve. "I will if you will."

"Seriously, what if Preston found it?"

Leanna turned toward the mirror to twist her hair in a bun and secured it with a pair of combs.

"Something tells me I haven't finished giving Van Slyck what he has coming to him."

Her hand clenched reaching for her bonnet.

Luckily, Cleve dashed out of the bedroom door without noticing that her fingers shook ever so slightly when she placed the hat on her head and plunged the hatpin home.

"I'm feeling a bit poorly to go out," Aggie mumbled.

"Nonsense, girl." Dorothy straightened Aggie's shoulders and pinched her chin between her fingers. "It's time you quit your moping. We've all been where you are. If Miss Leanna says we need to practice decorum at the general store, that is what we will do."

"Who knows? Along the way some handsome

prince…or farmer might sweep us off our feet."
Cassie pressed her fingers to her modestly covered
bosom and sighed. Her blue eyes stared past the
stained-glass window of the saloon as though she
could see him waiting for her to come outside.

"You better get your head out of the clouds, miss,
if you don't want to end up back where you started."
Lucinda tugged at her starched collar.

"It happened for Massie."

Leanna bent over to pick up Cabe, smiling because
it had happened for her, too. She would not have
dreamed it possible, but her mind was forever filled
with pictures of her naked prince, who admired her
to no end.

"No one is going back to where they came from,"
Leanna pointed out. "And if we don't happen along
any princes we will at least get some peppermint
candy."

"Cand!" Cabe clapped his chubby hands.

The walk from Leanna's Place to the general
store was short and much too direct. The weather
this morning was a step away from heaven, with one
foot still in summer and the other inching toward
autumn.

Even though some of them were not comfortable with it, she led her students on a stroll about
Town Square, then back toward the road to Fort
Ridge and the general store. She felt like a mother
hen herding her chicks through the hazards of the
barnyard.

To Cassie's clear disappointment not a single farmer showed his princely face.

A few folks gawked openly, but surprisingly, a few more merely ignored them.

Doc Lewis crossed the square to greet them, bless his soul. The ghost of a smile shadowed Aggie's eyes. Well, a prince had shown up, after all.

A moment after Doc Lewis crossed back to the other side of the street, Leanna sensed malice aimed smack between her shoulder blades.

This sensation was different from the one she normally felt in town. Chances are it was Preston peeking from behind corners.

Leanna shook off the uncomfortable feeling. There was nothing to be done about it. If he knew that she had tried to break into the bank, he didn't know that she knew that he knew. She still held the upper hand.

And really, it could be that Preston hadn't found the bracelet. He might simply be angry that the ladies were slipping out of his grip.

Or perhaps Preston wasn't lurking at all. Because of the missing bracelet, she might be imaging threats where none existed.

She had just led her brood in front of Rosa's Boutique when the door to the general store opened and Minnie Jenkins stepped out, only yards away.

Leanna spun about and gathered her chicks about her. "Do exactly what I do. Say exactly what

I say, and no matter what happens be proud of yourselves.

"Mrs. Jenkins!" Leanna strode forward with her hand outstretched and her smile beaming. "It's lovely to see you."

Minnie Jenkins, always poised, forever refined, stood like a deer caught gazing down the barrel of a hunter's gun.

Leanna pumped Minnie's hand up and down. "Please tell Ellie that I miss her and I look forward to calling on her."

Minnie's lips drew tight against her teeth. "I most certainly will no—"

Lucinda stepped forward to grasp the stricken Minnie's hand. "Mrs. Jenkins, it's lovely to meet you."

Mrs. Jenkins tried to wipe her hand on her skirt but it was taken up by Dorothy, then Massie and Cassie. Each of the ladies greeted her with wide smiles and wishes to make the pleasure of Ellie's acquaintance.

By this time Minnie looked as though she might faint dead away on the boardwalk. Now was the perfect time to press Aggie forward.

"Minnie," Leanna said, holding the reluctant Aggie about the waist and pulling her forward. "This is our Aggie. I'm sure you've heard the things that Preston Van Slyck has been saying about her. Most of them were never true and the things that were true no longer are."

Henry Stokes stood in the doorway, his pale blue eyes shifting between Leanna and Minnie. He gripped a broom in his hand and pretended to sweep. The man was a gossip. No doubt embellished tales of this encounter would be the talk of the town until a new tale came along.

Minnie swayed on her feet. Dorothy slipped a steadying arm about her shoulder. Aghast, Minnie yanked backward and tumbled into the arms of Lucinda, who set her upright.

"Do have a care, Mrs. Jenkins," Lucinda cooed in exaggerated concern.

Speechless, maybe forever, the shocked woman stomped away.

"You did beautifully, ladies." Leanna beamed at her charges. She turned to Henry Stokes, whose bushy brown hair stood on end more than it usually did. "A round of hard candy for everyone, Henry."

"Yes…certainly, Miss Leanna. I'll bring that right out. And there's a letter from your brother Quin."

"No need to bring anything out, we'll come inside," she answered.

"But… That is, these women?"

"I, for one, need a new hair ribbon," Cassie announced, and strode inside the general store.

Leanna couldn't recall when she'd been so proud.

Hearts for Harlots would be a success in spite of the Mrs. Jenkinses of Cahill Crossing.

Nothing that Preston Van Slyck and his crew

could do would stop her girls from the respectable lives they longed to lead.

Cleve stood several yards from where Leanna knelt between her mother's grave and her father's. He stood quietly with his hands folded in front of him while his wife spoke to her mother like there was not six feet of dirt and eternity between them.

She clutched the letter that she had received from Quin to her breast. It was creased with wear, having been opened and refolded a dozen times or more. His wife had even stuffed it into her corset and carried it close to her heart all last night while she worked.

"Mama," Leanna said, spreading the letter open to the grass over the grave. She shook her head and showed it to the headstone. She pointed it upward, then smiled at the cloud-dappled sky.

"Look at this! Chances are you already know, but Quin gave Cleve and me a wedding gift. Land, Mama. He gave us a portion of the 4C. I'm coming home! Cleve and I, little Boodle and..." She glanced back at him. She whispered something to her mother that he didn't hear.

"Aggie's doing a bit better and the other ladies are coming right along," she chatted on.

While Leanna discussed the progress of her chicks, Cleve let his mind wander over the spread of land he and Leanna had just visited.

It wasn't as harsh as the land he had farmed before. Quin's gift was acre upon acre of rolling hills with fresh clear streams running through it. The turf was green and the sky so blue it hurt his eyes to look at it.

Earlier this morning they had decided where to build their house. They'd made love there, in the grass, with the sun warming their bare flesh, welcoming and blessing them.

Leanna had just told her mother she was coming home. Well, by damn, so was he.

A couple of months ago he had been a man with two things on his mind. Claim his sister's boy, then get revenge on the monster who had ruined her.

Today he was a family man. He had a wife, a child and land. He ought to be as content as a toad in mud on a hot summer night. Just one thing stood between him and his future with Leanna.

Lies.

While Leanna spoke with her mother, sunshine glinted in her black hair. Curls tumbled down her back with bits of grass and dried leaves stuck in them, witness to their lovemaking.

She turned her pretty face to smile up at him, her eyes sparkling. Leanna Holden, his wife, had changed his life. He could never go back to being the man he was before. He didn't want to.

Truth settled in his soul, as soft and certain as a feather drifting to the earth. He could try and deny it but all that would do is make him a bigger fool than he already was.

The day might come that Leanna found him out

to be a liar; hell, it probably would. But between now and then he would not lie about this.

"Leanna." He strode forward, then knelt beside her on the grass. "I have something to tell you and I want your Mama and Papa to hear it."

Cleve cleared his throat. He looked up, nervous. Maybe dead people actually could hear him. "Mr. Cahill, Mrs. Cahill, I'm in love with your daughter."

He looked away from the cloud he had focused on. Leanna stared at him, covering a gasp with both hands.

"I love you, Leanna." He tugged her hands away from her mouth and kissed it quickly. "I only wish I'd told you sooner."

"Some words never come too late." She cupped his cheeks with gentle fingers and kissed him back. "I love you, too."

Wrapping her arms around his neck, she pressed against him so tight that he felt the patter of her heart, a heart that he would rather die than break.

"Cleve, I'm afraid to breathe I feel so lucky."

"Go ahead, love, take a deep breath. I'll always be here…I'll always love you."

He stood, lifting her with him.

Leanna glanced at the sky, following the changing shape of the cloud. "You were right all along, Mama."

"I'm taking your daughter back to town, Mrs. Cahill," he said. "But I'll bring her home soon."

"I think it's all right for you to call her Mama now."

"Forgive me for being dense as a board," he crooned into Leanna's blush-pink ear. "I was yours from the first time I saw you bleeding all over the back porch of the saloon. I was just too dim-witted to know it."

Leanna sighed with contentment; every bone and muscle rejoiced. She strolled about the saloon barely feeling the floor under her feet.

Cleve loved her.

With her parents' deaths and the family disintegrated by hateful words, there had been a time when she'd feared her life might be shattered beyond repair.

But Cleve loved her. Now she had everything she had ever dreamed of...and a tiny something more.

The breeze gusting through the open front door threatened to scatter winning and losing hands to the floor. She crossed the room to close it, smoothing the gathers of her skirt over her belly as she went.

With her hand on the doorknob, she watched leaves tumbling across the road. Rocking chairs on the front porch tipped back and forth with no one in them.

A shadow moved in the street, then a young woman, clearly from across the tracks, stepped into the lamplight. She dashed up the stairs, glancing backward over her shoulder.

"Miss Leanna, I need your help." She hugged her arms across her middle, shivering in her skimpy gown.

"Please, come in."

"Oh, no, I couldn't." She glanced behind her again. "I'd like to speak with you…in private. Can we walk a bit?"

"I'll get my husband. We'll be safer—"

"Oh, please!" The clearly distressed woman clutched Leanna's elbow and drew her onto the porch. Lanterns swayed, squeaking on their hooks and shooting light in erratic patterns into the night. "I'll only take a moment of your time…leastwise, I have to get back before I'm missed."

The poor woman kept ahold of her elbow, tugging her down the steps. Her trembling made it impossible for Leanna to refuse her.

"We could just talk over there…on the other side of the road." She anchored her blowing red hair with her free hand while she gripped Leanna's elbow, tugging her along. "There's that big bush. We can stand behind it and no one will see me. I won't take but an instant of your time."

"If someone is threatening you, we can help." Standing behind the shrubbery out of sight of the saloon was not a position she would have chosen, but apparently there was no help for it.

"I'm sorry." The girl spun about. She ran, her hair blazing behind her, a flicker of crimson in the night.

"Really, Leanna, you're wasting your time."

Preston stepped into view, his grin feral for all its attractiveness.

"You won't be able to help them. They're mine,

even Aggie…especially Aggie." He drew something from his suit pocket. "I'll have her back and soon."

"Not against her will, you won't."

She watched him twirl her bracelet around his thumb. It glittered in the moonlight.

"She and the other whores sold their free will the first time they opened their legs for a dollar."

"If that's what you came to say, you've wasted your breath." She turned to go back inside, being careful not to look overlong at the bracelet.

Preston snatched her wrist and dropped the gold circle in her palm.

"It's very pretty, but I doubt you came to offer me a gift. Not that I would accept one from you, anyway, the way you treat those unfortunate women across—"

"It's yours and you know it. You dropped it behind the bank the other night."

"Someone may have, it wasn't me."

"Your initials are on it."

She peered closely at it as though she had never seen the lovely bangle.

"L…C," she read slowly. "It might be Lonnie Carter's, or maybe Libby Cole's." She prayed that Preston didn't feel her pulse racing in her wrist. She was frightened being alone with him. There was no telling what he might be capable of. "They would have lost it during daylight hours, though."

Boldly, she picked it up with her free hand and dropped it back into Preston's coat pocket. Regret nearly made her pluck it out again. Chance's gift had always been special to her. More than a common piece of jewelry, it represented the bond with her brother.

"You ought to ask Libby. She would be heartbroken to lose such a pretty thing." Sadly, Libby was the sort who would claim it as her own in a heartbeat.

"You're quite the pretty liar, Leanna." He squeezed harder on her wrist. "Tell me, what the hell were you doing? I know the Cahills aren't so destitute that little sister needs to break into the bank.... So, what, then?"

"That's a question for Libby...or Lonnie." She shrugged as though she didn't care. "Let go of me."

"Or what? You'll call your husband to come and rescue you? I'm shaking in my boots now."

She kicked her foot and connected with his shin.

He made an arrogant *tsk-tsk* sound so she aimed for his groin but only snagged the crotch of his trousers.

"Now, now, no need for violence." He squeezed harder. "Although, I do enjoy a hellcat on occasion. Another time, maybe. For now, all I want to know is what you were up to behind the bank."

"Leanna!" Cleve's voice carried across the road from the front porch.

Preston released her. He took a long backward stride.

"Watch the little things you hold dear," he hissed.

Her breathing stilled. She flushed head to toe with

cold dread because, very clearly, he did not mean the bracelet.

She ached to run across the road toward Cleve and safety but she would be damned if she would let Preston see her fear. She took slow, measured steps even though her back ached with the venom being stared at her from behind.

What felt like a hundred years later she reached the safety of the steps.

"What were you doing alone in the dark?" Cleve's voice sounded relieved.

She stepped into the arms that he held out to her. She pressed her cheek against his chest and felt his solid body wrap her up.

"I wasn't alone."

"Van Slyck?" Cleve spoke the name like it was refuse in a garbage heap.

She nodded against his silk vest. "He's going to give my bracelet to Libby Cole."

"Go inside and close the door." Cleve let go of her and turned as though he meant to dash back across the road.

"Wait!" She latched on to his sleeve. "I know you want to give him what he deserves. But right now he only suspects we were up to something. If you go after him, he'll know it."

"He'll know not to approach my wife again."

"Please, Cleve, wait just a little longer."

"All right, for now…" He slipped his arm about her waist and ushered her into the saloon. "For the sake of finding out if he and his father know anything about your parents. But one day soon, Leanna, I'm going after that man and I'll ask you not to stop me."

"I won't want to."

Chapter Twelve

Agreeing to allow Van Slyck to slither away, a serpent in high grass, had been difficult. That decision ate at Cleve and left him restless through the night.

"Take Boodle out riding," Leanna had suggested to him as they finished breakfast. "He could use some fresh air."

"Come with us. We'll make it a family outing."

"Papa always said that men need time to just be with men, even if the men are pint-size."

Since she was right, he had saddled up Fey, who according to his wife also needed an outing, and taken his son on a ride.

The wind had blown away with the dawn leaving behind a perfect day to show off Cabe's new home to him.

Sunshine touched Cleve between the shoulder

blades. He stretched, easing some of the tightness out of his back.

"Fshn." Cabe sat in him front of him with his boot toes tipped toward the sky. He pointed to a stream.

"As the years go by I expect you'll spend a lot of time sitting beside that stream, my little man." He ruffled Cabe's dark hair with his palm. "We'd take a ride over and thank your uncle Quin for that, but he and your auntie are still away."

"Fshn," Cabe repeated.

"All right, but your mama says no hooks until you're a mite older."

Cleve dismounted and lifted Cabe from the saddle. He found a reed and tied a string that he found in Fey's saddle pack to it.

With the boy settled between his knees next to the flowing clear water, Cleve allowed some of his anger from the night before to wash away with the current.

A reckoning time would come, but it wasn't this fine sunny morning with Boodle chatting happily at the string bobbing about in search of hidden fish.

"Arden would be pleased to see you here." Someday, when Cabe was older and able to understand, he would tell him about her.

Arden had made the right choice in giving her son to Leanna. With every day that passed, he was more thankful for his sister's decision.

Cleve hated the fact that he had come to Cahill

Crossing with the intention of taking the child away from Leanna.

He tried to imagine Arden's face smiling down at the pair of them sitting here. It was easier than he would have thought. One day he might speak with her the way Leanna did with her mother.

The no-good man that his sister had been involved with still needed to be dealt with, but not on this fine day.

Besides, he didn't know who the man was. Trying to force Leanna into telling might earn him a bed in the pantry behind the kitchen.

For as long as she wanted to keep the secret of Boodle's daddy, he wouldn't force it from her.

That didn't mean he wouldn't try to find out on his own.

"Come on, son, let's go sit up on that great big rock and see what there is to see."

"See!" Cabe leaped up and dropped his crushed willow pole.

Cleve lifted him and carried him on his shoulders up the boulder. It was an easy climb with deep chunks of rock hacked out for easy assent.

Apparently, this place had been visited before, many times. He supposed Leanna knew of it.

He pictured her as a child, maybe skinny with knobby knees, her hair in braids while she tagged about after Chance. It could be that the two of them sat in this very spot.

Chance and Leanna had been close; he'd heard story after story of them growing up.

She worried about this brother. Chance ought to have picked up the letter from Mrs. Jameston in Deadwood by now. Too many times he'd caught his wife listening for the train whistle, or watching the road.

"Horsee!" Cabe pointed to a herd running in the distance.

He wiggled, trying to launch his small self off Cleve's shoulders.

"It's a long fall from here." He secured both arms about his squirming son.

Son…it was a good word. Day by day, that's how he felt. Less of an uncle and more of a father.

Cabe looked up at him with sunshine falling full on his face.

"Go horsee!"

His eyes, wide and pleading, were as blue as his mother's. Leanna might have given birth to him, the shade was so close. What was all his own was the gold fleck in the blue. It resembled the moon when at its half, with a dot at the tip that looked a bit like a star.

Cleve liked to think that he got it from a Holden ancestor. He wouldn't allow that his son had gotten a single trait from the bastard who hadn't stayed around long enough to know that he was a father.

"Lets go, then, Boodle. Let's see if Fey can catch up with that herd and give you a better look."

* * *

Leanna watched the pulse tick in her brother's cheek.

"I'm in charge of law and order around here." Bowie drummed his fingers on his desk, glaring at her, then at Cleve. "You can't just waltz in here and announce that you didn't have any luck breaking into the bank."

Leanna leaned forward in the chair across from him. "I don't know why you are so upset. It was you who asked me to gather information."

Sitting beside her, Cleve shook his head.

"You can't blame your brother. What he asked is that you listen, not gather."

She shot her husband a severe frown.

"As I recall, you were already breaking into the bank when I got there."

"Only to keep you from doing it." He smiled at her, of all the nerve! "Besides, I'm not the one who promised to stay out of trouble."

"The only reason you know about that promise is because you were eavesdropping." She could scarcely believe that Cleve was taking her brother's side.

Bowie slammed his fist on his desk. "The pair of you are lucky you didn't get inside the bank. I'd have had to arrest you."

Annoyed, she snatched her glare from Cleve and settled it on Bowie. "You wouldn't arrest your own sister."

"I'm the law. I'd be obligated to."

"In that case you…" Leanna bit off her words. She had nearly blurted out that, as the law, he was obligated to find out who killed Mama and Papa and had failed to do so. She had come within a breath of reverting to that selfish girl who had argued with Mama that last day.

It wasn't that Bowie didn't need arguing with, but he didn't deserve to have hurtful accusations hurled at him.

"Here, now." Cleve smoothed open her clenched fingers. "We can discuss this and settle some things, or we can argue and not."

Bowie nodded.

Leanna shrugged because while she was willing to listen calmly, and even discuss some things, she was not willing to stop doing whatever she could to find the murderers.

"Bowie was right," Cleve said to her. "It was a mistake to break into the bank."

He turned his attention on Bowie. "But I have to tell you, brother, listening for clues is worthless. Van Slyck sits in his chair and chats with his buddy Fitzgerald most evenings but they don't talk about anything more revealing than the weather or the charms of widow Greenly."

"We came here this morning to inform you of our progress," Leanna said. "I just want to let you know that there is none."

Bowie stood, his arms anchored across his chest. "And I want you to know that you're off the case."

"Bowie, I respect your right as a lawman to say so." Cleve stood, as tall as her brother, engaging him eye to eye. "But Leanna has a right to know what happened. I'll do my best to keep her out of trouble, but we are going to continue to try and find out."

Leanna rose. She presented her back to her brother and her smile to her husband.

"I love you, Cleve." She pressed a kiss to his cheek, then walked around the desk to Bowie.

She kissed his cheek. "I love you, too. Even if you are more like Quin every day."

"What is that supposed to mean?"

"Think about it, King Bowie."

Cleve touched her waist and guided her to the open door.

"Annie, you are second in command here and when I say your job is to... Oh, hell." Bowie was silent for the moment it took them to cross the threshold.

"Holden, if anything happens to my little sister I'm taking it out on your hide."

Thanks to Massie, Cleve's hide remained safe from Bowie, for the time being, at any rate.

He stood outside the church this crisp Saturday morning relieved that a wedding had kept Leanna too busy to hunt killers.

Scarcely an hour after they had left the marshal's office last week, Massie and Sam had paid them a call. Sam had begged Cleve's permission to marry his one and only true love…the very next day.

He had given his blessing without hesitation. Leanna had not.

According to Leanna, Massie would be wed with music, flowers and a gown to make her groom weep. Not in a hasty rush like they had something to be ashamed of.

With the ceremony just finished, Sam's eyes were damp, along with Leanna's, Lucinda's, Cassie's and, he couldn't deny, his own.

At one time Massie may have been labeled a fallen woman, but with Leanna's help she had learned to stand. This morning she emerged from the front door of the church a glowing bride.

Only one person equaled her for radiance. Leanna followed her fledging, showering her with flower petals as she came down the church steps with her new husband.

The newlyweds stopped to kiss.

Leanna snatched up the lacy hem of her skirt and hurried across the grass to him, her face flushed pink with victory.

He couldn't recall when he'd seen her more beautiful.

"Hearts for Harlots did this!" She hugged him about the middle, then leaned back to gaze at his face. Her eyes reflected the pure September sky.

"You did this." He ran his thumb along the curve of her smile, as proud of her as she was of Massie.

"In two hours our Massie is going home. I feel like dancing a jig." She spun about. A froth of violet lace whirled about her. "We still have a couple of hours to celebrate before the train leaves."

"I spent half of last night thinking about the reception at Steven's Restaurant." He smacked his lips. "Nice rare steak, mashed potatoes, succulent berry pie."

"Oh!" Leanna covered her mouth with both hands. She looked suddenly pale. "I'll meet you there."

She hurried around the side of the building. She must have remembered some important wedding detail that she had forgotten, some decoration or frill in Steven's dining room.

Cleve lifted Cabe from Dorothy's arms and carried him the short walk to the restaurant. Happy chatter surrounded him. For a couple of hours he would try and forget that his own young marriage was based on a lie and very possibly doomed as a result.

"Melvin Wood!" Dorothy called. "You leave that pup be and come back here!"

Melvin dashed into a stand of trees behind the church trailing a big shaggy mutt.

"Oh, that boy," she huffed.

"If he catches it will you let him keep it?"

"That would be your decision, Mr. Cleve. It's your house he would be bringing it to."

"A house needs a dog." The more he considered it, the better he liked the idea. Dogs wagged tails when family approached. They bared teeth and snarled at strangers.

When they reached Steven's Restaurant, Leanna waited for them on the front porch, her smile bright and welcoming.

The feast, joyous with many toasts, was halfway finished when Melvin dashed in the front door. He glanced at Cleve, then Leanna. His unhappy expression indicated that he had not caught the dog.

He hurried to a shadowed corner of the room where he slid onto a chair and slumped, staring at the floor until a whistle announced the arrival of the noon train.

The wedding party grew silent for a moment. Leanna looked at Massie, Massie looked at Leanna. Everyone stood because the train wouldn't wait on their goodbyes.

As a group they escorted the newlyweds the short distance to the station. Tears streamed down the women's faces to puddle in the creases of brave smiles.

It might be a long time, or forever, before Massie saw her friends again.

The groom twisted his hat in his hands and apologized to Leanna for being one of the folks who had scorned her upon her return to town.

Leanna hugged Sam and Massie, one arm about each of them. She whispered something in Massie's ear.

The whistle blew again, a signal that the locomotive was ready to pull away from the station.

The Webbers boarded the train only a moment before the big wheels moved on the rails and a rush of steam poured out from under the engine.

As one, they waved and watched until the train was a speck of smoke in the distance.

"Mr. Cleve." Melvin tugged on his arm. "There's something I've got to tell you."

"What is it, son?" The child looked miserable.

Leanna touched his forehead the way women do when they are hunting a fever.

"It's just…" Melvin glanced sideways at Leanna. "Can this just be between men?"

"I reckon that would be fine." He arched a brow in question at his wife. She answered with a nod.

Cleve walked away with Melvin while the rest of the group turned for home.

"You didn't eat anything earlier. What do you say we get a bite of whatever smells so good coming from the baker's oven?"

Melvin shook his head. "My belly's not right."

"Is something troubling you, son?"

Melvin reached into the pocket of his pants and withdrew a dollar bill.

"I didn't want it." He pressed the bill into Cleve's fist, then wiped his hand on his pants. "But if I didn't take it, I figured the man would think I knew he was up to no good…must have figured me for a simpleton."

It was Cleve's turn to look around.

"What man?" He gripped Melvin's shoulder and tugged him closer.

"Don't know who he was, but he was hiding in the trees when I went after the dog. He caught me by the arm and said he meant me no harm." The boy glanced back over his shoulder. "I figured he wouldn't have been hiding behind a tree if that was true."

"You ought to have called for help."

"Wouldn't have found out what he was up to if I did."

"Did you find out?"

Melvin nodded. "Said he'd give me that dollar and another one later if I'd bring Cabe to the stream where it cuts behind that old elm at the schoolyard. Claimed he has a present for him," Melvin said in a rush. He gulped a deep breath. "He told me to come tonight when everyone's asleep. I didn't want to let on that I was shaking, but I was that scared of him. Miss Lucinda always says that just because a fellow looks like a gentleman doesn't mean he is. I expect he was one of those."

He was exactly one of those.

"Thank you, Melvin. I'll take care of him." Cleve squeezed his shoulder. "I think it's better that we don't mention this to the women."

"I figured you'd know what to do." Melvin leaned in close to Cleve.

He didn't, exactly, but come dark he'd figure it out.

"What happened to the dog?"

Melvin shrugged one skinny shoulder and sighed.

"I nearly had it but it ran off when the dandy threw a rock at it."

"I suppose a boy of your age wants a dog pretty bad."

"More than anything, Mr. Cleve." Melvin kicked a clod of dirt and sent it rolling.

"Soon as I can, I'll get you one all your own."

Melvin stood a bit taller. Freckles crinkled over his nose when he grinned.

"What will I do with the dollar? It's tainted."

"That would only be true if you'd done what the man wanted. As I see it, you can do whatever you want with it."

"Miss Leanna says money ought to be put in the bank so it can grow. I heard her tell Dorothy that she put the money her brother Chance sends her from his bounties in an account so it can be his when he wants it. He doesn't know it, though, so it will be a surprise."

"You and I will pay a visit to the bank Monday morning. That dollar can be the start of whatever you want it to be."

"A horse—I reckon that's what I want."

Concealed behind a shrub that grew between the stream and the appointed elm, Cleve watched Van Slyck cross the schoolyard. He strode toward the tree wearing his customary black evening suit.

In the deep shadow of the witching hour he might have been mistaken for a drifting spook had it not been for his clumsy footsteps. Cleve figured inebriation was rare in a specter and Van Slyck was well into it judging by the way he swaggered.

"Good lad." He lurched toward the figures sitting at the base of the tree. "Wasn't sure you'd show."

He crouched and plucked the sleeve of Melvin's shirt. The fabric shifted and a hank of straw stuffing fell out of the neck. He shook Cabe's short trousers with the same result.

"Don't play with me, boy." Van Slyck stood, gripping the limp dummy in his fist. He turned slowly in a circle, scowling and scanning the shifting shadows of the playground.

"If it's more money you're after, bring your little friend out here and I'll double it."

Cleve wanted to leap out of the bush and throttle Van Slyck, but he kept still. Who knew what he might reveal, believing that he was babbling to Melvin?

Still, it was a challenge to keep his voice from roaring in outrage and his fists from plowing into Van Slyck's gut.

Not only was the man a bully to the women across the tracks, he had forced Cleve to deceive his wife. Leanna, making up for his absence at the saloon, believed that he was home in bed with a bellyache.

The lie was half-true, now that he thought about it. His belly did ache with the need to give Van Slyck what he had coming.

He'd have to wait on that, for now at least. Push Van Slyck too far and Leanna might never discover what he knew about her parents' deaths, if he knew anything.

For Leanna's sake, Van Slyck would get away with a warning, but it ate at him.

"All I want is for the little fellow to give his mother a message. I won't harm either one of you...you have my word." Van Slyck inclined his head, listening. "As a gentleman."

Cleve shook a branch of the shrub and Van Slyck's head whipped around.

He wove his way toward the bush, nearly stumbling with a drunken misstep. He spread the vegetation aside, looking down to where he must assume the children hid in terror.

Cleve reached up and grabbed him by his knotted tie. Van Slyck hit the ground hard on his knees.

Nose to nose with him, Cleve watched the coward's eyes widen. In the dark, the speck in his iris that he had noticed earlier shimmered like a gold nugget.

Cleve's temper burned so hot that it was hard to see clearly. He stood, yanking Van Slyck up with him. His free hand curled into an impatient fist.

He thought of his wife and the in-laws he would never get to meet. He pictured them in his mind and jammed his fist against his thigh.

"What's the message, Van Slyck?"

He sputtered. The coward tried to pry Cleve's fingers from his tie.

"What? Too yellow-livered to deliver it man-to-man?"

Van Slyck cursed. Cleve hauled him up, then dragged him to the stream. He tipped him backward over the water.

"Last chance to get it off your chest," he said.

"Damn those Cahills, every last one of them. Damn you, double."

"That's what I figured."

Cleve let go of the tie and Van Slyck fell backward into the stream. Dropping this fool on his ass was becoming a regular occurrence.

"Keep the hell away from my family or next time I won't be so gentle on you."

Chapter Thirteen

Monday arrived along with the first day of fall. Cleve stood on the front porch of Leanna's Place with a mug of coffee between his palms enjoying the crisp air nipping at his face.

Leanna sat in one of the rocking chairs with a shawl across her shoulders. She appeared a bit pale but she smiled up at him.

"Summer left in a hurry," she said. "Boodle, stay away from those stairs."

Cleve blocked a possible tumble with his knee and directed the toddler toward his mother. She scooped him up and settled him on her lap, wrapping the ends of the shawl around him.

"Here comes the wind." She turned her face into a fledgling gust and took a deep breath. "There's something exciting about the weather changing, don't you think?"

"There's something exciting about watching you become excited."

If he could steal her away to the broom closet right now, he would. But inside the saloon, the place was a hum of activity. The ladies, Aggie included, dusted, swept and scrubbed the main room in preparation of the coming week.

"Looks like you're feeling better...hungry, even," she murmured with a seductive arch of one brow.

"Starved, in fact." He hadn't made love to Leanna since his belly issues, just to make the lie more convincing. "You look like you might be catching it, though." Not from him clearly, but she didn't seem quite herself.

"I'm taking Melvin to the bank this morning," he said. He set his coffee mug down on the porch rail and traced his thumb along the curve of her cheek. No fever, at least. "The boy earned a dollar the other day and wants to save it for a horse. We'll take Boodle along with us so you can get some rest."

"I'd rather keep him here with me." Leanna stood, tucking the shawl tighter about Cabe.

"Let him come." Leanna rarely took Cabe into town. It was time his world expanded. "The boys will have a good time."

She shook her head. "He'll only get fussy."

The wind gusted harder by the second and the temperature dipped with it. To Cleve it was invigorating after the long, hot summer, but maybe she was right. Cabe would be better off staying here where it was warm.

"Let's go inside, then. I'll gather up Melvin. As hard as he's scrubbing the floor, he might have another dollar to go toward that horse."

Half an hour later, Cleve walked into the bank with Melvin hopping up and down beside him. The boy was clearly proud of opening an account of his own. Every tenth step from home to here, he had suggested a new name for the steed he would own someday.

"I reckon Black Ace would suit him," Melvin declared, reaching up and sliding two dollars across the counter.

By a stroke of luck, Willem worked alone this morning. Cleve might have had a hard time not leaping over the counter to finish his business with the younger Van Slyck.

Involved at his desk, Willem dipped his pen in an ink bottle, scribbled something on the bottom of a sheet of paper. He looked up, smiled, then rose from his desk and crossed the room.

"What can I do for you, Mr. Holden? This isn't your usual banking day."

"Melvin would like to open a savings account."

"Someday I'm going to buy me a horse." He would reach that goal, if the eager expression on his face was anything to go by.

"That's a fine thing, young man. Start now and when you're ready you'll be able to."

The banker's smile at Melvin was as cordial as any he would give to a grown customer. He didn't look like a killer, just a common businessman with a son who might or might not be one.

He would dismiss Van Slyck as a decent man stuck with a detestable son, but he'd learned something over the past couple of months. Looks could be deceiving. A ruined reputation might hide virtue and a respectable facade might disguise wickedness.

He glanced about the bank as if a clue to what had happened to Leanna's parents might leap into the palm of his hand.

It didn't. Polished desks sat upon waxed floors. The place smelled like old leather and almond. To all appearances nothing questionable took place between these walls.

The big iron safe in the back was locked as tight as the secrets that the Van Slycks might keep.

With the transaction completed, Willem shook Melvin's hand, then Cleve's.

"Until this evening, then, Mr. Holden."

A shaft of morning sunlight shot through the front window and illuminated the banker's face. It glinted off his eyes.

Cleve's heart stopped. His stomach heaved. Damned if his soul wasn't writhing on the well-kept floor.

Preston's eye, blue and gold… Willem's eye, the same. Father and son, both with identical half-moons with a star at the tip.

Breathe, he told himself, in and out, even and

steady. Stand straight…smile…act as though the world hadn't just quit spinning.

"Is there something wrong?" Van Slyck withdrew his hand from Cleve's. He flexed his fingers.

He must have clamped too hard on the older man's hand without being aware of it.

"Not at all." He forced a friendly, casual smile. "It's just… I hope I'm not being forward in asking, but you and your son have the same unique eye coloring."

"That's how I know he's mine." Van Slyck shrugged. He smiled, lifting one side of his mouth. "Couldn't disown him even if I tried to. All the Van Slyck men carry it, for as long as anyone can remember."

"It's a handsome mark," he managed to say when all he wanted was to puke on his boots.

He clasped Melvin's hand, crumpling the receipt that the child held proudly. He turned for the door and placed one foot deliberately in front of the other.

It made sense now, why Leanna usually left Cabe behind when she went to town.

The family mark *was* handsome, at least on Cabe.

Leanna sat at her dressing table absently brushing her hair. Looking in the vanity mirror she watched Cleve's reflection while he sat on the bed.

Something fascinating must be happening on the floor. He'd been staring at it for a good long while. He claimed to be healed of his bout of stomach trouble, but he didn't look it.

Walking home from work in the wee hours this morning, he'd held her close, just like always, but now he was silent, brooding even.

Cleve never brooded.

All at once, his reflection stood and walked toward her. Bare feet whispered against the carpet while wind rattled the shutters that had been closed against the violent gusts. Twigs from the tree outside hit the slats, scratching and splintering.

From behind, Cleve kneaded her shoulders with strong fingers. He smelled like seduction, warm and male.

She leaned back into him; her purr of pleasure whispered through the room.

He gazed down at her in the glass. "You look like a goddess in that nightgown."

He flicked the straps off her shoulders, then plunged his hands between the sheer lace and her flesh.

"Goddesses are cold creatures." She covered his hands and pressed them closer to her heart. "I'm not a bit cold, Cleve."

"You know that I love you." He held her gaze in the mirror. He slid his hands out of her sleeping gown and pressed her shoulders. "That no matter what happens, I will always love you?"

"That sounds ominous." She pivoted away from

the mirror to look up at him. "But yes, I know you love me. No matter what happens I love you, too."

He strode to the middle of the room and turned his back on her. He studied the ceiling, which, to her, looked the same tonight as it had every night. He scrubbed his hands through his hair, then spun about to face her again.

Leanna set her brush on the vanity; she folded her hands on her lap. Cold air seeped through the window frame.

"I think you need to tell me what's bothering you," she said.

"I know that Preston is Boodle's daddy."

"Oh!" She stood, her stomach and her head in a spin. She rushed across the wool roses on the rug. "I'm sorry, Cleve."

She pressed her head to his chest and his arms came about her shoulders, hugging her tight. A tremor shivered through him.

"I should have told you, you had a right to know. But I made his mother a promise."

"I understand that." She felt his voice rumble under her cheek. "You were right to give his mama that respect. I'm grateful for it."

"Grateful? Why would you be?"

She peered up at him. His eyes had misted over but he shook his head, clearing them.

"Because she... I need to..." He took a long breath and let it out slowly. "I'm about to tell you something—to do something—and you won't like it. Hell, you'll hate me for it. But even then, try and remember that no matter what happens, I won't let Van Slyck take Cabe from you."

"I know that. I married you for it, remember?" She touched his cheek. "I haven't regretted that choice for an instant."

"You might… You will, dammit!"

She took a step back but held on to his waist. "Cleve Holden, what's gotten into you? I know you are upset that it's Preston, but it doesn't matter. Cabe has as much of his good mother in him as he does the man who fathered him. Besides, the man who did Arden wrong is not his father. You are his father."

"I'm his uncle." His eyes closed tight; he lifted his face to the ceiling. "Arden's last name was Holden. She was my sister."

All of a sudden, she needed to run to the outhouse and be sick. The floor seemed to shift beneath her. Why had he kept such a secret from her?

A sickening dread settled in her belly. She dashed away a searing tear streaking down her cheek. "Why did you marry me?"

It hurt to have her husband touch her tenderly and break her heart at the same time. She shoved him away, then inched toward the window, coming up against the vibration of the tempest against her back.

"Leanna, you are the best person I know. I reckon I owe you the truth." He sucked in a breath and held it for a moment. When he exhaled, it sounded like a groan. "I came to Cahill Crossing to take my sister's son."

Aching silence inside pressed against the fury outside.

"Why didn't you?" Anger, pure and hot, consumed her.

"I tried...I never could find the words."

"Since you were too cowardly to speak up, you married me? To take control of my son?"

He shook his head. "It wasn't as coldhearted as all that. The situation was so damned complicated, and Cabe was only part of the reason I married you."

"What's so complicated about telling the truth? I didn't ask for more than that." She heard the voice of a stranger coming from her mouth, catlike and hissing. Anger had never taken her so completely. "Cabe is a Cahill. I'll never give him to you!"

Why couldn't the earth just open up and swallow her? She stood at the brink of such pain and scandal that she didn't think she would recover from it.

"Here's the truth," he said, his voice sounding raspy in his throat. "I needed to marry you because of him...I wanted to marry you because of you."

How had she reached into the vanity drawer and pulled out her revolver without being aware that she did it? Luckily, it wasn't loaded because at this instant she really did feel like pulling the trigger.

"No more lies, Cleve." She pointed the weapon at him, anyway.

He sprung forward, then plucked the useless metal

from her fingers. He tossed it on the bed, then pinned her between the window and his chest, his fingers firm on her shoulders.

"Listen to me." His hateful words hit her in the face. "I didn't marry for love, you knew that. You didn't marry for it, either. But something happened between us and you damn well know it. I love you, Leanna. I will love you forever."

"Never say that to me again." She pushed against him but it was like shoving a boulder. "Next time I'll load that pistol."

"I'm sorry I didn't tell you that Arden was my sister. You can't imagine all the times I tried. But once I got to know you, I couldn't take your boy away. What could I do but marry you? I couldn't leave him…I couldn't take him."

She beat his chest with both fists. "Get out of my house!"

This time he had the decency to stand aside.

She ran to the bedroom door and flung it open. The wall behind it shook.

Her life shook, coming down around her with the knowledge that the man she had trusted more, even, than a brother was not who he had seemed.

Cleve Holden was a liar, a cad…and the father of the child growing innocently in her womb.

"Leanna!" Cleve stood below the bedroom window, bellowing. He cursed because the infernal wind snatched the sound away as soon as he opened his mouth.

All at once the shutters opened and she peered down at him through a rectangle of light. Midnight-black curls whipped about her face. Her breathing, angry and fast, made her bosom rise against her lacy gown. The very last thing his wife brought to mind was a cold goddess.

No matter how she cursed him, or rejected him, he would win this woman back.

She tossed something out of the window. His coat tumbled through the night to land at his feet.

He deserved every bit of what she gave him, but that didn't make it any easier to shiver out here in the dark.

An avalanche came out of the window. Shoes, shirts and undergarments fell on his head, then joined the coat on the ground.

"There's something you need to know!" he called the next time she popped her head out of the window.

"I've heard all I want to from you."

Now wouldn't be the time to tell her that he was going after Van Slyck. That he would see justice done for his sister's death.

Whatever knowledge Van Slyck had regarding Leanna's parents' deaths would be lost once he did what needed doing. She would hate him more than she did now once that had happened.

If there were another way he would take it, but sometimes in his dreams he saw Arden's tears. He heard her crying. He had no choice but to settle the score for his sister.

Since his wife didn't shut the window, but continued to glare down at him, he said, "I love you, Leanna."

"I told you before, no more lies." She clutched something in her fist but he couldn't see what it was. "You're going to need this."

She leaned out of the window and opened his money pouch. Bills tumbled out to be snatched away by the wind. Come morning, folks in town would find an unusual treat.

"And—" she cupped her mouth to make sure the words reached him "—you're fired!"

"You can't fire me from being your husband." A flying twig struck him on the head.

"I can when I divorce you." She began to slide the window closed. "Get out of my yard, get out of my life."

"I won't agree to that. You are my wife and Cabe is my boy. I'll get out of your yard, for now, but I promised to watch out for him and you, and hell if I won't do it."

"He's my boy, not yours! I managed fine before you came along. I'll do it, and quite nicely, again."

"Only a few minutes ago you said you'd love me no matter what."

"I said I'd love you. That doesn't mean I ever want to see you again."

"Well, by damn, you're going to!" he shouted.

She slammed the window closed and an instant later the bedroom lamp went out.

He gathered up his clothes, a one-dollar bill and his determination to reclaim his family. He walked toward the hotel listening to the loose shutters over Leanna's bedroom window banging in the wind.

Chapter Fourteen

Leanna came out of Arthur Slocum's office and shut the door behind her. She leaned against it and took a jittery breath.

Sadly, her anger at Cleve didn't dull the pain of his betrayal. She had hoped that speaking to the lawyer about a divorce would be the first step toward having her old life back.

The problem was, her old, scandal-ridden life was not what she wanted.

It would be coming back to her in spades, though.

If the good folks of Cahill Crossing thought she was wicked for bearing a child out of wedlock, they'd figure she was far beyond redemption when word spread that she was filing for divorce while pregnant.

No, she didn't want her old life; she wanted the bright future she had seen with Cleve.

She dashed a tear from her eye and hurried down

the steps. Just this minute she couldn't think about the ranch and the happy family that would never be hers.

Right now she needed to pick up her mail. Maybe there would be word of Chance. Perhaps he was coming home; she prayed he was coming home. She could tell her brother her heartache and he would understand.

Leanna entered the general store, wiping her eyes and striving to appear bright and friendly.

Her smile was wasted since the only one inside was Henry, who stood with his back to her holding an envelope to the light streaming through the window.

She cleared her throat. Henry tucked the envelope behind his back and turned around to greet her.

"What can I do for you, Mrs. Holden? I've got a shipment of bright new ribbons fresh off the train."

"Just my mail, Henry." It was a rare day that she didn't feel like purchasing a new ribbon. The clerk was bound to take note of it.

"Just finished the sorting. Nothing for you today." Henry pulled out the tray of ribbons, anyway. She pretended to be interested. "Some kind of weather we're having. That big blow last night! Some folks are saying we're in for something strange, weather-wise, that is."

"It is the time of year for change." Weather was a change she welcomed, but being forced to part with Cleve? That was a change that made it hard to find her next breath.

Anger, she was discovering, didn't heal a broken heart; it only glazed the wound over for short periods of time.

"Good day, Henry," she muttered, turning and walking toward the front door. She left it standing ajar for the customer entering.

"I'd like to speak with you." Cleve's voice came from too close beside her. Had she been carrying a package she would have dropped it, then tripped over it.

"Are you following me? Go away!"

"Only keeping an eye out." He glanced up and down the street. "You shouldn't be wandering about alone."

"I'm not wandering. I've been to see Arthur Slocum and spoken to him about the divorce."

"You wasted your good time, then. I'll be your husband until I breathe my last."

"Might not be long, as soon as my brothers find out what you did." She shrugged, but the thought of losing this man, for any reason, cut her heart. "Go away, Cleve."

She spun away and caught the shocked expression on Henry Stokes's face as he stood in the doorway.

"If you spread that rumor," Cleve said to the postmaster, "you'll answer to me, friend."

She stomped away. Fat chance Cleve's threat would do any good. No doubt at this very instant, Henry was relaying the news to half the town.

* * *

Tonight, Aggie was going to work. The bruises on her face had healed. Now it was time to heal her heart. That couldn't happen if she remained watching life parade by her from shadowed corners.

Leanna escorted her down the stairs whispering encouragement. They turned at the bottom of the staircase and entered the saloon.

Aggie gripped Leanna's elbow. "Men are staring at me."

Everyone was staring.

"It's because you look beautiful."

"I'm not sure I can—"

"Hush now, you can do this. You've practiced what to do. It's the same gentlemen here as always. They know the rules."

"What if Preston comes?"

"I don't think he will. He—"

"Don't worry about him, Miss Holt. I'm here," Cleve announced behind them.

Leanna smiled at Aggie and pointed her toward Lucinda, who laughed with a customer and poured him a drink.

Leanna spun about. "I fired you!" The nerve of the man, showing up anyway, and with a big handsome grin on his face.

"So you did. Tonight I'm volunteering." The crease in his cheek lifted. "And every night after this."

"I don't want you here."

"And I don't want a divorce." He reached for her

but she stepped beyond his grasp. "Come out back with me," he said.

"I will not!"

"I have something to say.... It involves your parents."

She had it on her tongue to tell him to report it to Bowie. Unfortunately, their conversation was attracting attention. And truly, she did want to know what he had to say.

"All right, but don't touch me. Don't even smile at me."

The man must have gone deaf...or addle-brained, because he reached for her. She walked quickly through the back room and out to the porch, keeping three strides ahead so she wouldn't become a victim of the pressure of his calculating fingers on her arm.

"Well, what is it?"

Cleve sat down on the top step, gazing out at the cloudy night.

"Sit with me, love."

She stood still and silent, glaring down at the top of his head.

"No, thank you, and I am not your love."

He cocked a brow. "I'm going to do something and you won't like it."

She backed up, ready to flee. She would not be lured by a kiss, if that's the trick he had in mind. She would never fall prey to those lying lips again.

"Will I like it less than the fact that you married me to try and steal my son?"

"I married you because I realized I didn't want to take him from you. And you know that's not the only reason." He looked up at her, not charming or seducing, simply looking miserable. "Won't you sit with me?"

She nearly did. The ache to brush against him and inhale the familiar scent of his skin was intense.

A mental reminder that this man was not the man she fell in love with kept her on her feet. Her Cleve had been helpful and honest. This Cleve was a deceiver, however appealing he remained.

"Whatever unpleasant thing you have to say, just say it. I have a saloon to run."

"I am going to make Van Slyck pay for what he did to my sister."

"He deserves it."

"I'm going to do it tonight."

Stunned silent for a moment, she gaped at him.

"My parents deserve justice as much as your sister does." How could he even be considering this? "Whatever Preston knows dies with him, you know that."

He nodded. "And I'm sorry for it."

"I wish I could hate you. I'm going to try very hard." She took a step toward the back door.

Cleve leaped to his feet and grasped her by the shoulders.

She twisted and pushed. Even a stomp on his foot didn't gain her freedom.

"This has to be done now. There's better reason for it than settling the score, for Arden or your parents."

She attacked his shin.

"After Massie's wedding, Van Slyck tried to pay Melvin to bring Cabe out of the house after dark."

"I don't believe you!" She did, of course, but she was capable of keeping her son out of harm's way until she discovered what Preston might know. She had protected him from the moment he'd drawn his first breath, well before Cleve Holden had appeared on the saloon's back porch.

She would have aimed her knee at his groin, but a display of anger was useless against this mulish man.

"I'm asking you to wait." She showered him with her most winning smile. She sighed, and her bosom heaved. Perhaps charm would dissuade him from his reckless goal. "Just a while longer."

He shook his head. "Ask me anything but that."

How had she let herself marry such a strong-willed man?

He let go of her shoulders but slid his hands down her arms. He drew her forward. He lowered his mouth toward her lips.

That was one of the ways he had trapped her into marriage. She turned her face so that his mouth grazed her cheek.

"Please, Cleve, wait until we find something out. After that, I don't care what you do with Preston. Have Bowie lock him up for a hundred years! Just, please…wait."

He released her. She backed up against the wall.

"Maybe I owe you that…as much as I owe Arden her justice." He walked to the back door and paused with the knob in his hand. "All right…for now. But I'll be moving back into the house."

"You will not! We're getting divorced."

Stubborn was the nicest thing she could say about him. Stubborn and perceptive. He had a way of looking too hard at her, as though he could see inside her soul. She didn't want him there.

"Here's something I've noticed about you Cahills," he said. "It's easier to ask for forgiveness than for permission. I'm coming home."

"I won't forgive you and I won't let you in my house."

Why, the nerve of the man, shrugging his shoulders before he went back inside the saloon. He left the door standing wide open behind him.

Curse it! She certainly would hate him…if she could.

Leanna shivered even though the air being pressed between the weighty clouds and the earth was warm.

Out there in the night was a man who would do a child harm. A man whose secrets she had to discover before he had the chance to act.

A new gown wouldn't heal Leanna's pain, but it might take the edge off for a moment.

For a precious hour this morning, she had time to herself. With Cabe tucked safely away at the saloon and all the ladies watching him, she felt comfortable enough to venture out. No doubt her infernal, soon-to-be former husband was there, as well.

She tried to enjoy the stroll to Rosa's Boutique but the air was humid and stifling. The cloying warmth made her want to gag.

Walking past the bakery didn't help. What used to smell divine now made her stomach heave.

And it wasn't only the baked goods making her queasy. Doubts had begun to flip her belly. Sympathy for Cleve of all things!

He'd lost his sister. Leanna had lost her friend. Cleve wanted to raise his nephew, his only flesh and blood. Any decent person would want the same.

But in the end, a decent person would have told her the truth right off, not have taken her heart only to break it.

Several more steps brought her to Rosa's front door, out of the range of forbidden aromas, but not grievous thoughts.

In the instant she would have gone into the boutique two women came out of the general store, only thirty feet away—Minnie and Ellie.

"Something's not right," Minnie declared, and sniffed the air with her pert nose. "Everyone says the weather is bound to turn foul in a way we've never seen. Mark my words, Ellie."

"Mother, you make too much of it." Ellie turned and spotted Leanna. "Annie!"

"Ellie Jenkins, you will not speak with that woman.

You heard what Mr. Stokes said." Minnie latched on to Ellie's sleeve. "She's divorcing her husband. I won't have your reputation tarnished."

"If our Annie is divorcing her husband I'm sure there is a very good reason for it."

Ellie yanked free of her mother and rushed toward the boutique. She wrapped Leanna in a great hug and rocked her back and forth.

"I couldn't be happier to see you," her friend whispered.

The sound of Ellie's voice made years fall away. The pair of them were young girls again, laughing at life and full of hope. Mama still waited on the front porch with open arms. The spotless reputation that made her the darling of one and all remained untarnished. Broken women didn't call out in her dreams for help. The love of her life hadn't betrayed her.

Tears stung her eyes. Her lungs ached with the effort to hold them in. She might have let them flow freely had Minnie not been glaring daggers at her daughter's back.

"No matter what, I'm on your side," Ellie murmured in her ear. "I'll defend you to anyone, Annie. I don't care what Mother has to say about it."

"That means everything to me, especially now." She hugged Ellie's slender shoulders, clinging to the past for all she was worth, and then she let go. "Your mother is right, though. You have your future to think about. You'll want to marry a solid, respectable man soon. That can't happen if you're seen with me."

"Oh, piffle, Leanna!"

Ellie kissed her cheek, then returned to her mother, to all appearances the obedient daughter she had always been. Clearly, though, Ellie had begun to stretch her wings.

Minnie would soon see a side of her daughter that she wouldn't approve of.

She watched Minnie and Ellie walk away and prayed that the price of Ellie's budding independence wouldn't ruin the relationship between them. Minnie could be harsh and proud, but in the end, she was a living, breathing mother. And Leanna knew what it was to want the best for your child.

By pure luck Cleve found what he believed to be the perfect dog for Melvin. It was a huge beast that the widow Greenly could no longer care for, being half as tall as the widow and a near match to her in weight.

When he had come upon Mrs. Greenly clutching an empty rope in her hand and watching while the animal happily romped from one end of Town Square to the other in only a matter of seconds, he had offered to buy the beast.

Mrs. Greenly had snatched the dollar bill from his hand and replaced it with the rope.

In the fifteen minutes that he had owned Stretch, he was pleased with the purchase. A dog this size would be a protector. It wasn't clear what Stretch's pedigree might be. He was tall, lanky with a deep chest; his sleek fur was gray and dappled with black, except for his feet which were white and shadowed by dust.

"Melvin and Cabe might try and ride you," he warned Stretch as they strolled toward the home that Cleve had been banished from. "You do resemble a cow."

Soulful, saggy brown eyes peered up at him.

"All right, a horse." The dog swished his long dappled tail.

From close by, someone hammered a piece of wood over a window, apparently fearing whatever might be coming with the clouds. The sound echoed sharply across the road.

Startled, the dog jumped and glanced behind him.

"Not you, too." Cleve patted the knob on top of the dog's wide head without having to reach down to do it. "What do you think? Hail the size of cow pies or the Cahill Curse? I've heard that and a few other things."

Stretch answered with a soft "Woof."

"Here we are, boy. Between the two of us, you, at least, have a shot at getting inside."

Facing the front door, Cleve figured he had a right to walk right in, but he knocked.

On the other side of the panel he heard light footsteps cross the floor. Leanna's, he was certain.

She opened the door.

"I've brought Melvin his dog," he announced before his wife had a chance to slam the door in his face.

"That, Cleve Holden, is no dog." She reached her hand toward Stretch's floppy ear. "It's a co—"

"Stretch prefers to think of himself as a horse."

With her hands on her hips, Leanna studied the dog.

"In any case, I don't have a stable."

"Stretch is a house dog. He's partial to a soft couch from what I've been told." He couldn't help it, his wife's scowl made him grin.

"Take yourself and your beast off my front porch."

"It's not my beast, its Melvin's."

"Go away." She began to close the door but Stretch nosed his way inside. True to his reputation, he headed for the couch. He sat down on it.

That's where Melvin discovered him a few seconds later, with his hind quarters on the cushion and his paws on the floor, looking very humanlike in his pose.

The bond between the boy and his dog happened faster than a blink.

While Leanna considered the happy scene taking place a few yards away, he stepped inside and shut the door behind him.

"I reckon the dog is staying," Leanna said. "But you are not."

At that point Cabe dashed into the room looking for Melvin.

He hurried to Cleve and yanked on his pant leg. He pointed to Stretch. "Horsee, Papa!"

"You'd better leave. I don't want my son getting false ideas about riding dogs and you being his papa."

"There's nothing false about me being his papa. Nor about the way I love him, or you."

"Everything is false about that, Cleve. It was from the very first day."

Stretch lifted up from the couch and trotted to Leanna. He slid his head under her hand, then leaned against her, forcing her to correct her balance.

"You've tricked me into keeping this mammoth, now leave my home."

"The lie I told you was wrong, I know that. I'll respect you by leaving these four walls. But not the front porch. I'll be easy to find if you need me."

Stretch gazed up at Leanna, his soulful canine eyes full of devotion.

"That's the most foolish thing I ever heard," she exclaimed.

It probably was, but he went outside and plunked down in a rocking chair. Miles away lightning crackled over the horizon but was too far away to make a sound.

The front door slammed. This was shaping up to be a very long wait.

Chapter Fifteen

The next day, the still-distant flashes of lightning had folks jumping at shadows. They shuttered windows and bolted doors. The Cahill Curse coming home to roost, the whispers went.

Tonight, the saloon had seen only half the number of patrons. She had been forced to close up an hour early.

Simpleminded nonsense.

She opened the door to the upstairs bedroom where Cabe and Melvin slept. Stretch, lying on the floor between the beds, opened one eye at her and wagged his tail.

She covered Cabe's shoulders with a blanket, then did the same for Melvin before going to the window and drawing back the curtain.

She peered down at the porch. At two in the morning it was utterly dark outside. She couldn't see a foot beyond the windowpane.

Just then, lightning scattered across the horizon to illuminate the porch in flashes and flickers.

Stubborn man. Earlier, Cleve had followed her home from the saloon. She'd shut the door in his face and insisted that he spend the night in a hotel. Still, there he sat for the second night, squeezed into a chair and watching for goblins and criminals who might pop out of the darkness.

Did he think that acting as a human shield would get him back inside? That it would make her believe that he loved her, after all?

It would not! She was well aware that he was only sitting down there for Boodle's sake. If Cleve were free to take the child, he'd no doubt be far from Cahill Crossing and all its trouble by now, no matter that he promised that he wouldn't. Truth was not Cleve's strongest virtue.

Another flash revealed him twitching in the chair. It couldn't be comfortable, sitting and staring at nothing for hour upon hour.

For one thing, she had taken the cushions inside. For another, he was too large for the chair's woman-size frame.

Bullish man. Balancing that rifle over his knees for half the night had to be a strain.

She let the curtain fall back in place.

"No disrespect to you, Stretch. I'm sure you are a fine watchdog. But the pitiful truth is, and I wish it wasn't so, I will sleep better because he's out there." She patted the big, solid head. "Good night, then."

She smothered the bedroom lamp, closed the door, then walked into the hall. She snuffed out a lamp on the hallway table, then tiptoed to another window overlooking the porch.

She gazed down in time for a brilliant flare to reveal that Cleve was now shivering.

She had no call to feel sorry for him. His uncomfortable condition was his own choice.

A choice he had made for her safety, an unwelcome voice in her mind reminded her. Because, the voice pestered on, he claimed to love her.

She went downstairs to bank the parlor lamp.

She snatched a blanket from the couch, then sat down and covered herself with it.

Wrongheaded man. Her Winchester hung over the mantel, loaded and ready to be fired. Protecting Boodle was her job, not his.

She ought to fire the weapon at Cleve. At his feet anyway, just to get him off her front porch.

She pictured him limping away, finally accepting that she would not forgive him. And why would he even want the forgiveness of a woman he'd never wanted to marry in the first place? What difference would it make?

The one and only thing the man wanted was his nephew and she knew a very good way to point it out.

She stood, shrugged the blanket over her shoulders and strode to the front door. Once Cleve acted in the way she knew he would, she would be free of him.

There was the chance that he might set a lawyer on her to try and take her Boodle away. It was a certainty, though, that she would set her brothers on him.

Opening the door, she stepped out into the darkness. Fractured light illuminated Cleve's face.

Difficult, handsome man. If she were to be completely truthful, she'd have to face the fact that she would miss the way his hair dipped over his forehead in a brown swirl. In every man's smile from here until forever, she would see that crease in his cheek and remember how it flashed in flirtation and mischief.

She'd try her best not to pine for the way he always looked past her face and saw her soul. He knew things about her that no one else knew.

"You win." She tossed the blanket at him. "You can take Cabe anywhere you want. Just go away."

She wouldn't give her son up, not in a thousand years. This was simply a way of proving his intentions. Once he demonstrated those, she would be free to kick him out of her heart as well as off her front porch.

Cleve was quick. One instant he was lounging awkwardly in the chair and the next he had her pinned to the wall, pressing her in place with his belly and hips.

"I won't take that child from you and you damn well know it." He held her shoulders against the wood slats, his palms hard and tense. "What's your game?

Have your brother arrest me for kidnapping on my way out of town?"

"I told you, you can have him."

His breath panted against her face, hot and quick. She had to close her eyes because even in the dark she saw his expression. Frustration, anger and—this she knew even with her eyes closed—sorrow.

He caught the hair behind her ears and tangled his fingers in it. He lifted her face and pressed the tip of his nose to hers.

"I'm not going any damn where without you. I won't quit my job and I won't quit your porch."

She pushed her hands against his chest to shove him away, but she let them rest over his thudding heart because, suddenly, she wasn't sure whether to shove or yank.

"You are the most stubborn, bullish, wrongheaded, purely difficult male I have ever known."

"That must be why I'm going to kiss you. You can forgive me later."

She yanked. He lifted her with the kiss. Lightning struck the night and for the first time in days she heard far-off thunder. It trampled across the sky and rumbled in her veins.

Cleve pressed her to the wall with his hips. He lifted the hem of her shift, kneading her thighs and spreading them.

"You know that I love you." He nipped her earlobe. The heat of his breath scorched her resolve. The pure male scent of him stole inside her. It invaded and conquered. "Admit it, Leanna. Tell me you know it."

"You are persistent beyond reason." She hadn't meant to moan that, but with night pressing in black as pitch, her senses intensified. All she could do was feel. Feel his hands caressing her waist, then stroking the curve of her hip. Feel his hard body shifting while grinding her to the wall.

Feel the truth…acknowledge it.

"I know it." The admission didn't break her. She thought it would have. "I know you love me."

He cupped her bottom with his nimble gambler's fingers. Lifting her, spreading her, he plunged home. She clenched about him but he didn't respond to the slide of her hips.

"Do you forgive me, love?"

She answered by rocking against him.

"Say the words."

"I forgive you." She fell apart from her heart outward. "I'll always love you, Cleve."

He took her and shattered her. Now and forever he owned her love…and her trust.

When the world gathered once more around her, she found that she was sitting in his lap while he rocked her in the too-small chair.

"I expect I should have said this a few moments back," she murmured. She nuzzled her nose into the crook of his neck to inhale the scent she had missed. "Won't you come inside?"

"Now that you mention it, I believe I will."

He reached down. In one fluid, powerful male movement he stood, carrying her in one arm and the shotgun in the other.

On the safe side of the door, he kicked it closed with his boot.

The bed blurred before Cleve's eyes. He fell face-forward onto it.

After two nights spent sitting on the front porch staring out into the dark, his head felt like lead, his eyes like sockets full of sand.

Now, with the ones he loved behind locked doors, and Stretch to keep watch over the boys, to listen for things that humans couldn't hear, he closed his eyes.

He felt his boots being yanked off, then the trousers that still sagged around his hips.

Soon he was bare, his wife naked and velvet-skinned beside him.

He tucked her into the curve of his belly and she wriggled her bottom in close to his groin. He'd feared that he would never share that intimacy with her again.

Leanna spoke but he was too weary to make sense of the words. Still, the sound of her voice seemed like a lullaby soothing away life's troubles. He floated in and out, cloudlike, hearing a word here and another there but not making sense of anything.

He smiled when he heard her mention *ranch*. That dream loomed before him more precious than ever. *Child* flitted through his mind. When his voice would work again, he'd tell her about his dream of a passel of sky-eyed, dark-haired brothers and sisters for Cabe.

That would be something for her to talk to her mother about.

He felt a kiss brush his forehead.

"I never quit loving you, Cleve."

And she never would. He'd spend his life making sure of that.

"Stretch, come out from under the table." Leanna offered the dog a biscuit left over from breakfast, but he whimpered at it. "A strapping fellow like you ought to be fearless in protecting the house."

Expecting Stretch to protect the house from the unrelenting bolts of lightning scattering over the land was unreasonable. No doubt, dogs all over town were hiding under tables.

"Boodle, baby, come over here and sit next to Stretch."

Cabe leaped upon the dog's wide neck and squeezed. "Horsee."

"He's a dog, remember? A horse wouldn't lick your face like that." Or be cowering under the furniture. "Since you're going to grow up on a ranch, you'll need to know the difference."

Cleve ought to be home from escorting Dorothy and Melvin to the train station shortly. They would all feel a bit more courageous then.

Hearts for Harlots had seen another success when

Dorothy had felt worthy enough to contact her cousin who lived only an hour's train ride away. The cousin had children Melvin's age who were excited to meet him. Luckily for Leanna, Dorothy had chosen not to move closer to her cousin, but to remain in Cahill Crossing, to continue to work for them when they moved to the ranch.

A sudden bolt of electricity flashed so close that it must have struck in town. Thunder rattled the house.

Leanna jumped and covered her thumping heart with her hand but Cabe gazed calmly up at her.

"S'at, Mama?"

"It's called lightning, the sound is thunder."

"Big," he commented, then stroked Stretch's nose.

Ten minutes later a fist pounded on the door.

"Thn'd," Cabe told the dog.

Leanna pulled aside the curtain over the window beside the door.

"Just Uncle Bowie," she said, and let him inside.

"Better come quick—lightning hit the roof of your place. The ladies are plenty scared."

"As scared as that?" She indicated the dog under the table while she gathered up Cabe.

"Not quite." Bowie lifted Cabe from her arms. "Leastwise, they're not under the table yet."

Bowie's big horse carried the three of them to town in under two minutes.

She had expected to see a few curious folks come to inspect the damage, but not a crowd. And most certainly not Preston, going from person to person, whispering.

Carrying Cabe up the front steps with Bowie behind her, she heard Preston commenting on the Cahill Curse.

Interfering gossip. He was worse than the postmaster. At least the postmaster talked about everyone. Preston meant to cause grief to her alone.

"Move along home, folks," Bowie ordered. "It's not safe to be standing out in the open."

"Marshal, come quick!" a voice called from the street. "The jail's just been hit!"

"Maybe they're right, we are cursed." Bowie kissed her cheek, then ran for his horse.

The crowd followed Bowie. Apparently, the prospect of escaping, or at least incinerated, prisoners was of more interest than frightened former harlots.

"What was our damage?" Leanna asked Lucinda while she handed Cabe to Aggie.

Aggie remained in the saloon while Leanna followed Lucinda and Cassie upstairs.

"The roof of the top bedroom is singed but it didn't burn," Lucinda answered.

Leanna hurried up the stairs to Aggie's top-floor bedroom. Smoke puffed from the blackened point where the rafters peaked but it grew fainter while she looked at it.

But if rain came with this lightning storm there would be some damage.

"I've got to get Boodle back home before it begins

to pour. Maybe you can get some buckets to catch the drips. Push the furniture up against the walls just in case."

"We'll take some of it downstairs." Lucinda dragged a quilt from the bed and Cassie gathered up the pillows.

Leanna snatched a pair of chairs and carried them with her to the second floor. She set them in the common area between the bedrooms, then descended to the main saloon.

Preston stood in the center of the room. He held Cabe in his arms. Aggie had apparently fled.

"Put my son down!" Leanna demanded, but a hit of thunder dulled her shout.

She rushed forward and Preston lifted Cabe beyond her reach. He stared at Cabe's face, into eyes that were a perfect match to his...and his father's.

"Who is his mother?" For once Preston's suave manner deserted him. His eyes locked on Cabe's as he settled him to his chest and rubbed his hand over the dark curly head.

"I am. Give him to me before I have you arrested."

"Better think that over," he said without looking at her. "It's you who will be arrested. I'm simply a wronged father. Kidnapping is a serious offense. Even your brother won't be able to let that pass."

Frightened, Cabe struggled to wriggle out of Preston's grip.

She couldn't fly at her enemy like she wanted to,

biting and scratching. She had another tiny life to protect as well as Cabe's.

"You won't be able to prove that. He looks as much like me and Cleve as he does you."

"Holden?" He looked at her for the first time. "Adel? No…Arden, wasn't it? Yes…sweet little Arden Holden. She was a treat. Whatever happened to her?"

"You killed her."

"Tsk now, she was alive and well when we parted company." Not a shadow of sorrow spoiled his angelic expression. "That does leave me free to take my son home to his proud grandpappy, doesn't it?" Cabe began to cry.

Leanna wanted to scream for help, but what might Preston do if she did? Silence her in a way that would hurt her unborn baby?

"Give him to me. The last thing you want is a child."

"As true as that may be, my father will be—"

Suddenly Preston went limp. He sagged to the floor, gasping. Leanna snatched Cabe before he hit the rug.

Aggie stood over the groaning devil with a frying pan gripped in both fists.

"Give him another wallop, then get the others out the back way," Leanna instructed.

She ran, hugging Cabe to her. After only a block, her lungs burned and her legs ached. Keeping hold of him was possible only because her arms were cramped in place. Even though she thought one more step might break her back, she pushed on, worrying all the while her flight might be hurting her precious unborn baby.

Rain slammed the front porch the second she opened the door and launched herself into Cleve's arms.

Chapter Sixteen

"Come here, son." Cleve lifted Cabe from her arms but she couldn't straighten her elbows. "Go sit under the table, son. Help Stretch be brave while Mama catches her breath."

Cabe pumped his short legs toward the kitchen. He crawled under the table and sat on the dog's back.

"What's wrong?" He led her to the couch and eased her down beside him, rubbing her back in slow circles. "Breathe slow...easy now."

"Preston knows," she gasped.

His hand stilled on her back. "About Cabe?"

She nodded, nearly too breathless to speak. "His eye."

"It had to happen someday." He resumed stroking her back. "I don't want you to worry."

She would, there was no help for it, but with Cleve close by she did feel safer.

He stood up from the couch and paced to the fireplace. He plucked the Winchester from the wall, checked to see that it was loaded, then placed it back on its hanger.

"Lightning hit the saloon, we had to go," she told him when he resumed his place beside her. "Bowie was with us then, but later, somehow Cabe got away from Aggie and there was Preston holding him and saying how pleased Willem would be when he brought the boy home."

"You weren't hurt?"

She shook her head. "Preston was. Aggie walloped him in the face with a frying pan."

"Killed him, I hope."

"I reckon she wanted to, but she couldn't, not without ending up in jail herself." Leanna took a shuddering breath. "I'll never believe that man wants to be anyone's daddy."

"He hopes to redeem himself in his father's eyes through Cabe, no doubt."

"He's more a fool than we thought if he believes that will happen. Willem will think even less of him for having a child the way he did."

"Preston's a twisted man. Who knows what his father is?" Cleve hugged her and whispered in her ear, "He won't get our boy and neither will Willem. I promise you that. Lay down." He pressed her onto the cushions and lifted her legs, smoothing them to the couch. "Rest awhile. I'll see to Boodle's noon meal."

With a kiss to her forehead, he stood, then walked

to the window. He tapped on the glass, peering out at the heavy rain. After a moment, he returned to the hearth and checked the rifle one more time.

"What are you going to do?" she asked.

"I'm going to give Boodle something to eat." He looked down at her, more grave and severe than she had ever seen him. "When Van Slyck comes, I'm going to kill him."

"But, Cleve, you promised—"

"Everything has changed since then."

He was right. Now that Preston knew about Cabe, the rules had changed. Protecting their son trumped every other consideration.

Still, Cleve couldn't just shoot Preston. Bowie would call it murder. The law wouldn't allow for the man deserving it.

She closed her eyes, thinking of what could be done. Lightning flashed; she watched it brighten beyond her closed lids. Thunder vibrated the house time after time.

Maybe Stretch had the right of it. They all ought to crawl under the table.

She cracked her eyes open in the same instant that the front window shattered, the sound muffled by thunder.

A slender, feminine hand dropped a dripping sheet of paper inside, then withdrew.

She hurried to the window and snatched the note from the floor.

Preston, it read, *was holding Aggie, Lucinda and*

Cassie. He would hurt them unless Leanna brought Cabe to the saloon within five minutes.

From here, it would take ten minutes. No time to send for Bowie.

The man was a fool if he thought she was taking Cabe anywhere. She ought to show Cleve the note and let him take care of Preston. He wanted to…and badly.

But Cleve would kill him. He would be convicted of murder. She would lose her husband again, to prison—or the hangman's noose.

Besides, what if Preston was trying to lure Cleve away from home? Leaving her and Cabe unprotected in the house might be his plan.

In either case, she could not tell Cleve, and chances were, the ladies were perfectly safe. Preston only mentioned them as a lure. He might be mean but, as far as she knew, he wasn't a killer.

Since there was only one way to know, she stepped onto the front porch and dashed down the steps.

Several yards down the road a dim, wet figure emerged from a flailing bush. Preston caught her around the waist and smothered her scream with his rain-slicked hand.

"If it's not the widow Holden? Pretty Leanna, you really are too easy."

A woman screamed. The sound of her fear filtered through the downpour.

Cleve dropped a biscuit spread with raspberry preserves on the table in front of Cabe.

He lunged for the back door. Leanna had been resting on the parlor couch only moments ago, he was certain.

He flung the door wide to see a soaked stranger standing several yards beyond the bottom step of the porch, her red hair streaming water.

As soon as she spotted him, she closed her mouth and ran.

Stepping outside, he called to her. Something slammed his skull. He hit his knees.

When the darkness receded from his mind and consciousness trickled back, he found himself in motion, crawling into the kitchen with blood dripping past his eye to pool in the corner of his mouth.

He sat back on his haunches, then spat on the floor.

The room spun; it tilted and rolled. Van Slyck stood beside the table appearing to tick-tock. He clutched Cabe in the crook of his elbow while the child pummeled and screeched.

"Got something you want, Holden?" A wicked-looking grin spread across his face. "Ah, but make that two. Clumsy of you to let your wife slip away."

From his position on the floor he peered into the parlor. Leanna was no longer on the couch.

Clearly gloating over his successful scheme, Van Slyck failed to notice the lumbering form silently creeping out from under the table behind him.

"I've got everything you hold dear, Holden. But then, I always have."

Van Slyck did notice when Stretch chomped his great mouth around his elbow. The dog growled. A deep rumble echoed off the walls. Huge teeth clamped and held.

Pinned in place by Stretch's jaws, evidently stunned by his predatory stare, Van Slyck screamed. He dropped Cabe.

Cleve lunged forward and caught him. Still unable to stand, he dragged Cabe backward and shoved him into the large pantry closet.

Cleve whistled even though it seemed the effort would explode his head. The dog let go of his terrified victim.

Stretch backed toward the pantry flashing his canines, drooling and growling. He plunked down on his haunches, blocking Cabe from view. Cleve slammed the door.

He needed to stand. It would be impossible to defend his position before the pantry while on his knees. Once Van Slyck quit trembling he would regain the advantage.

Cleve pushed up, inch by painful inch. He pressed his back against the door, willing his legs to support him. He wouldn't lose this battle to protect his wife and his son. He wouldn't waste this opportunity to avenge Arden.

Muscles stiff, knees locked, nausea swallowed, he rose and stared Preston down.

"Out of my way, Holden."

"Go through me."

"I could blow you over with a sneeze." He arched one brow. The dark, slick hairs formed an arrogant curve. "But I'd rather do it like this."

The gun that Van Slyck withdrew from the waistband of his pants was a wicked thing that looked as though it had been polished in honor of this occasion.

Van Slyck drove his balled-up fist and the butt of the pistol into Cleve's belly. Pain shot bone-deep, then rippled to his throat. It buckled his knees.

He fought the downward slide. It was no use. His legs might have been mud instead of flesh and bone for all the good they did him. Splinters from the wood door gouged his shirt and his back as he pressed against the inevitable.

He watched the barrel of the weapon follow him down.

"Not so high-and-mighty now, Holden. How does it feel to be the one on the floor this time?"

"Better than it feels to be you," Cleve gasped. He thought he would vomit. He focused on the pain ripping his belly to hold him in front of the door. "That skillet gash made a mess of your pretty face. Won't be so easy to charm the ladies now."

"I charmed the bloomers off your sister...I'll do the same to your wife. She'll resist at first, that's her better-than-everyone-else way. Just so you know, I've got her tucked away sweet and tight. Sure, she'll fight me like a cornered cat, but in the end she'll come around. There's the boy—she'll want to protect him."

"I'm going to kill you, Van Slyck."

The gun drew closer to his face. Only inches separated him from a hole in the brain.

"It'll have to be from the great beyond, then. In another minute you'll be a ghost."

"Boo!" Cleve had the satisfaction of seeing the coward twitch.

He lifted to a crouch, with the door supporting him from behind. On the other side of the wood, Stretch began to howl in a low, eerie lament that was much more spooklike than "Boo."

"Better be a quick shot. The dog's after blood." Another twitch. Cleve grinned when the gun wavered from the center of his forehead. "You won't be his first."

"Shut up, Holden." He readjusted his aim and sopped a bead of sweat from his brow with his sleeve. "You'll die in another minute but I've got something to tell you...a little something for you to take to your grave."

The grin that had broken so many hearts became an ugly sneer. For once, the man's rotten soul shone through.

"Has to do with the better-than-anyone Cahills. I know you and the slut were looking for something that night at the bank." He giggled. If Cleve hadn't already been holding down his bile he would have had to do it now, the high-pitched sound was that repulsive.

"Father Dear is bringing the Cahills to ruin, little by little. Has been for a while, too. Old man's too dense to think I'm on to him, though." Again, the giggle. "That damn family won't have a penny left what with daddy keeping two sets of books and filching the Cahill rents."

He pressed the barrel of the gun to Cleve's forehead.

"That's not all by half. Take this with you. My father knows about the day—"

A shadow dashed across the hallway.

Leanna, a sodden dripping mess, stood with the rifle from the fireplace braced against her shoulder.

"Drop the gun, Preston." Her order was delivered as calmly as a daily greeting.

Van Slyck lifted the weapon from Cleve's forehead. He spun toward Leanna.

Cleve hurled his weight against Van Slyck's knees in the same instant that the Winchester's blast shook the walls.

Van Slyck slumped facedown on the floor. Blood pooled from under his vest. One blank eye stared in perpetual shock at the ceiling.

Leanna launched herself into Cleve's arms. Kneeling, she buried her face into his chest and wept. He rocked her and soothed her, whispering in her ear that she was the bravest woman ever born.

An instant later Lucinda and Aggie rushed through the parlor. They stopped in the doorway to the kitchen, dripping twin puddles on the floor.

"He had that coming," Lucinda stated, brushing lank hair from her face.

"It's hard to find a speck of grief." Aggie stepped forward and bent at the waist to peer closer. She shrugged, then stepped back. "Cassie went for your brother."

Bowie paced the parlor. Lucinda, Cassie and Aggie sat on the couch turning their heads while they followed his progress.

"Tell me, little sister, why there's a dead body on your kitchen floor."

Lucinda answered for her. "Because Cleve would be dead and that dear little boy would be kidnapped if he weren't."

Leanna glanced toward the top of the stairs. She listened. Thank goodness Boodle lay sound asleep in his room without ever knowing what had happened beyond the pantry door.

After shooting Preston it had taken a moment to feel life pulsing in her blood again. Once she'd been able to breathe again, she'd slipped into the pantry, covered Cabe's eyes and gathered him up. She'd carried him upstairs, sung him a quavering lullaby, then left him dozing with Stretch's long body dangling over the foot of the bed.

"He wasn't much of a man to begin with," Aggie noted.

"The world is certainly a better place for his loss." Cassie gave one curt nod. She crossed her arms over her bosom.

"Be that as it may, I need to determine if there was a crime committed," Bowie stated.

"Of course there was a crime." Lucinda stood and pointed her finger toward the kitchen. "Committed by him."

"So according to what Cassie told me on the way here, Van Slyck kidnapped Leanna and tied her to a tree."

Three heads nodded firmly in unison.

"After I whacked him with the frying pan, two times as Miss Leanna told me to," Aggie explained, "he lit out, cursing our boss in ways even I've never heard."

"We figured it best to follow him," Cassie added.

"And a good thing, too. He'd hog-tied her to that tree so tight she couldn't even scream." Lucinda glared at the kitchen even though the body wasn't visible from the parlor.

"Why would he do that?" Bowie rubbed his neck and glanced out the window. The storm had moved on, leaving a gusty wind behind. "I'll need a story to tell his father."

Leanna stood from where she sat on the arm of the couch, then walked over to Cleve, who leaned against the fireplace with one shoulder propped against it.

She checked the knot on her husband's skull before turning to Bowie. "It can't be the truth."

"What the hell's wrong with the truth?" Bowie bellowed.

"Let me just say," Lucinda stood before Bowie

with her hands on her hips, "Miss Leanna is the finest person walking the earth. If I were Arden I'd have done the same thing."

"Who in the blazes is Arden?" He settled his gaze hard on Leanna. "Annie, do I need to sit down?"

The ladies moved over to make room.

"That might be best."

Cleve touched her shoulder. He squeezed it, then he nodded.

"First of all," she began. "Preston found out who Cleve really was and came to kill him."

"Who is he…really? A couple of days ago it seems like you might have offered your husband to Van Slyck and saved yourself a divorce."

"I love Cleve with all my heart." She reached up to pat his hand. "Why would I divorce him?"

"Because you and every gossip in town said you were going to do just that."

She waved her hand in front of her face as though that incident had been no more than a pesky fly. "I changed my mind."

"Tell me, then, who is my restored brother-in-law really, and why would Van Slyck want to kill him?"

"Cabe's mother was my sister, Arden Holden," Cleve said, his voice sounding more than a bit husky.

"A dear friend to us all." Cassie sighed.

That confession made Bowie pop off the couch as though he had a spring in his pants.

"Annie? Is this true? You aren't the boy's mother?"

"Of course I'm his mother! I might not have given

birth to him but I'll fight anyone who says he isn't mine."

"Why didn't you just say so in the first place? You've put yourself through a hell of a lot of reproach for no reason. We'll have to begin a search for the boy's father," Bowie said, exactly the way she knew he would because of his obligations as marshal.

"As far as anyone outside of this room will ever know, Cabe is Leanna's own flesh and blood. So am I." With a knot the size of a plum on his skull and his posture hunched by the late Preston Van Slyck's attack, Cleve had never looked more of a hero.

"Cabe's father is dead on the kitchen floor." Leanna stepped away from Cleve and went to her brother. She covered his balled-up fists with her fingers, trying to soothe the tension from them. "Preston only made the discovery this morning. He came here meaning to take Cabe home to Willem. As soon as the girls untied me from the tree, we rushed here and I found him with a gun pressed to Cleve's head."

"Killing me was only the beginning of his plan. He had intentions toward your sister that you would have ended up shooting him for, anyway, Bowie." Cleve ran his hand through his hair and winced when he touched the knot.

Bowie nodded, the tick in his jaw pulsing like a heartbeat. "We'll have to make sure Cabe's grand-daddy doesn't find out about him."

Bowie walked out onto the front porch and closed

the door behind him. Silent, the five of them listened to his boots pounding the wood, back and forth.

Within a minute the door flung open and he came back inside.

"So, from what I can make of this mess," Bowie announced, "Van Slyck came here meaning to make Leanna pay for stealing the girls from his territory. I reckon it was Cleve who shot him. A man's got an obligation to protect his wife."

"It's true—he wasn't happy about Miss Leanna reforming us." Aggie folded both hands primly on her lap and nodded.

"Bowie." Leanna stood on her toes to hug her brother. "I'm sorry I brought shame on the family. There just wasn't any help for it."

"You could have come to me."

"You being the law, well, it muddies things. I couldn't have you looking for Cabe's family."

"Ladies?" Cleve asked, leaning away from the fireplace. "Would you mind fetching the undertaker?"

"That most certainly would be our pleasure." The three of them, still damp, but no longer dripping, hurried out of the house.

"Leanna, there's more that you and your brother need to hear," Cleve said.

"Oh, hell." Bowie resumed his place on the couch.

Leanna slipped down beside him.

"Van Slyck made a confession, or part of one before…" Cleve inclined his head toward the kitchen.

"It's what, or part of what, at least, we have been

looking for. According to Preston, Willem is keeping two sets of books on the Cahill rents. Apparently, good, respectable Willem is trying to bankrupt the family. There was something else he wanted to say but he died before he finished gloating about it.

"I have a strong feeling it may have been about your parents but we'll never know for certain. I'm sorry."

"I'm not sorry, Cleve." Leanna leaped up and rushed to him. She hugged his solid breathing chest tight and inhaled the scent of blood on his shirt. "Nothing he knew would be worth losing you."

"It can't stay hidden forever." Bowie slapped his hands on his knees. "Someone knows something and I'll find out what it is."

"Cleve and I are here to help."

"That, little sister, is what will leave me sleepless at night."

Leanna stood in front of her bedroom mirror combing her hair before getting ready for bed. Cleve stood behind her watching, his eyes warming in a way that made her want to finish the task in a hurry.

The flame in the lamp on the dresser cast the room in soft amber shadows. Outside, the September night had grown cold and still. Stars frosted the sky beyond the window with shimmering ice.

It had been four days since Preston's body had been carried from the kitchen. Enough time that she could tell Cleve about their coming baby without lingering gloom overshadowing the happy news.

"Make yourself useful and undo the buttons on the back of my gown." She winked at him. "I swear, it feels tighter by the day."

"I'm always here to lend a hand." He flexed his fingers, then slipped the buttons free. He shimmied the bodice to her waist.

"I've been thinking," he said, caressing her shoulders with firm, warm thumbs. "We ought to move out of this house."

"I agree. Whenever I go into the kitchen, I feel the echo of what happened." She thought that the shocking vision of a dead man on her floor might fade but it played before her eyes like a ghost.

She shoved the gown over her petticoats. A lavender puddle pooled at her feet.

"When I bought Stretch, Mrs. Greenly mentioned that she is going to Austin. Her house is only a block away," Cleve said. "Tomorrow, I'll speak to her about renting to us, just until we can finish a couple of rooms of our ranch house."

"How did we get so blessed, Cleve?"

"I reckon your Mama's got a hand in it…Arden, too."

A nightingale picked that very moment to twitter a tune on a willow branch outside the window.

"It's late in the year for nightingales," Cleve noted.

He watched in the mirror while she untied the

ribbon of her chemise. His eyes turned a warmer shade of brown. They always did when she undressed.

Even though talk about the Cahill Curse was stronger than ever, what with lightning striking both the saloon and the jail, and with the banker's son dying in her kitchen, Leanna knew that she was blessed.

"I want the ranch with all my heart." She stripped off the rest of her underwear and stood before the mirror naked. "But Hearts for Harlots will always be my calling. I can't give that up."

"I don't want you to." Cleve stroked the thickening curve of her waistline. "The ladies can run the saloon for the most part. We'll continue to help the women who want it."

"What do you see when you look at me, Cleve?"

"I see my life."

She took his hands and slid them from her waist to her belly.

"What else?"

"You look…" He skimmed both hands up her ribs, then flicked his thumbs over her nipples. "Darker?"

He stared down at her stomach, his ears turning pink with the beginning of a flush.

He slid both hands back to her belly. His fingers trembled.

"You look like you ate your dinner and mine, too."

He took her by the shoulders and turned her gently around. He kissed her for a long, tender time.

"If the baby's a boy I'd like to name him Chance," she murmured against his grin.

"That might work for a girl, too."

"You won't think that after you've met my brother. I like Arden Elizabeth."

"Will Chance be any easier on me than Bowie was at first?"

"Maybe not, you did steal away his baby sister."

"I didn't steal you, I won you. Not fair and square, I'll admit, but here we are." Cleve cupped her face in his firm, warm fingers. "And here we'll be, playing out our lives with a full house."

* * * * *

HISTORICAL

Where Love is Timeless™

HARLEQUIN® HISTORICAL

COMING NEXT MONTH
AVAILABLE JANUARY 31, 2012

THE LAST CAHILL COWBOY
Cahill Cowboys
Jenna Kernan
(Western)

RAVISHED BY THE RAKE
Danger & Desire
Louise Allen
(Regency)

THE WICKED LORD RASENBY
Marguerite Kaye
(Regency)

LADY ROSABELLA'S RUSE
Rakes and Rascals
Ann Lethbridge
(Regency)

REQUEST YOUR FREE BOOKS!

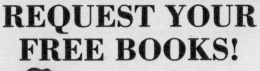

HARLEQUIN® HISTORICAL:
Where love is timeless

2 FREE NOVELS PLUS 2 FREE GIFTS!

YES! Please send me 2 FREE Harlequin® Historical novels and my 2 FREE gifts (gifts are worth about $10). After receiving them, if I don't wish to receive any more books, I can return the shipping statement marked "cancel." If I don't cancel, I will receive 6 brand-new novels every month and be billed just $5.19 per book in the U.S. or $5.74 per book in Canada. That's a savings of at least 17% off the cover price! It's quite a bargain! Shipping and handling is just 50¢ per book in the U.S. and 75¢ per book in Canada.* I understand that accepting the 2 free books and gifts places me under no obligation to buy anything. I can always return a shipment and cancel at any time. Even if I never buy another book, the two free books and gifts are mine to keep forever.

246/349 HDN FEQQ

Name	(PLEASE PRINT)

Address	Apt. #

City	State/Prov.	Zip/Postal Code

Signature (if under 18, a parent or guardian must sign)

Mail to the **Reader Service:**
IN U.S.A.: P.O. Box 1867, Buffalo, NY 14240-1867
IN CANADA: P.O. Box 609, Fort Erie, Ontario L2A 5X3

Not valid for current subscribers to Harlequin Historical books.

Want to try two free books from another line?
Call 1-800-873-8635 or visit www.ReaderService.com.

* Terms and prices subject to change without notice. Prices do not include applicable taxes. Sales tax applicable in N.Y. Canadian residents will be charged applicable taxes. Offer not valid in Quebec. This offer is limited to one order per household. All orders subject to credit approval. Credit or debit balances in a customer's account(s) may be offset by any other outstanding balance owed by or to the customer. Please allow 4 to 6 weeks for delivery. Offer available while quantities last.

Your Privacy—The Reader Service is committed to protecting your privacy. Our Privacy Policy is available online at www.ReaderService.com or upon request from the Reader Service.

We make a portion of our mailing list available to reputable third parties that offer products we believe may interest you. If you prefer that we not exchange your name with third parties, or if you wish to clarify or modify your communication preferences, please visit us at www.ReaderService.com/consumerschoice or write to us at Reader Service Preference Service, P.O. Box 9062, Buffalo, NY 14269. Include your complete name and address.

HHI1B

Louisa Morgan loves being around children.
So when she has the opportunity to tutor bedridden Ellie,
she's determined to bring joy back into the motherless
girl's world. Can she also help Ellie's father open his
heart again? Read on for a sneak peek of

THE COWBOY FATHER

by Linda Ford,
available February 2012 from Love Inspired Historical.

Why had Louisa thought she could do this job? A bubble of self-pity whispered she was totally useless, but Louisa ignored it. She wasn't useless. She could help Ellie if the child allowed it.

Emmet walked her out, waiting until they were out of earshot to speak. "I sense you and Ellie are not getting along."

"Ellie has lost her freedom. On top of that, everything is new. Familiar things are gone. Her only defense is to exert what little independence she has left. I believe she will soon tire of it and find there are more enjoyable ways to pass the time."

He looked doubtful. Louisa feared he would tell her not to return. But after several seconds' consideration, he sighed heavily. "You're right about one thing. She's lost everything. She can hardly be blamed for feeling out of sorts."

"She hasn't lost everything, though." Her words were quiet, coming from a place full of certainty that Emmet was more than enough for this child. "She has you."

"She'll always have me. As long as I live." He clenched his fists. "And I fully intend to raise her in such a way that even if something happened to me, she would never feel like I was gone. I'd be in her thoughts and in her actions every day."

Peace filled Louisa. "Exactly what my father did."

Their gazes connected, forged a single thought about fathers and daughters…how each needed the other. How sweet the relationship was.

Louisa tipped her head away first. "I'll see you tomorrow."

Emmet nodded. "Until tomorrow then."

She climbed behind the wheel of their automobile and turned toward home. She admired Emmet's devotion to his child. It reminded her of the love her own father had lavished on Louisa and her sisters. Louisa smiled as fond memories of her father filled her thoughts. Ellie was a fortunate child to know such love.

Louisa understands what both father and daughter are going through. Will her compassion help them heal—and form a new family? Find out in
THE COWBOY FATHER
by Linda Ford, available February 14, 2012.

Love Inspired Books celebrates 15 years of inspirational romance in 2012! February puts the spotlight on Love Inspired Historical, with each book celebrating family and the special place it has in our hearts. Be sure to pick up all four Love Inspired Historical stories, available February 14, wherever books are sold.